W9-CCI-544

THE
LÜNEBURG
VARIATION

A NOVEL

PAOLO MAURENSIG

TRANSLATED BY JON ROTHSCHILD

AN OWL BOOK
HENRY HOLT AND COMPANY
NEW YORK

Henry Holt and Company
Publishers since 1866
115 West 18th Street
New York, New York 10011

Henry Holt® is a registered trademark
of Henry Holt and Company, Inc.

Library of Congress Cataloging-in-Publication Data
Maurensig, Paolo.
[Variante di Lüneburg. English]
The Lüneburg variation / Paolo Maurensig;
translated by Jon Rothschild.
p.   cm.
ISBN 0-8050-6028-6
I. Rothschild, Jon.
PQ4873.A8947V3713   1998   98-34459
853'.914—dc21   CIP

Henry Holt books are available for special promotions and
premiums. For details contact: Director, Special Markets.

First published in 1993 by Adelphi edizioni s.p.a. Milan as
La variante di Lüneburg

First published in the United States in 1997
by Farrar, Straus and Giroux

First Owl Books Edition 1998

Printed in the United States of America
All first editions are printed on acid-free paper.∞

2   4   6   8   10   9   7   5   3   1

THE
LÜNEBURG
VARIATION

They say that chess was born in bloodshed.

Legend has it that when the game was first presented to the court, the sultan decided to reward the obscure inventor by granting any wish he might have. The recompense requested seemed modest: the quantity of wheat that would result from putting a single grain on the first of the board's sixty-four squares, two grains on the second, four on the third, and so on.

At first the sultan gladly agreed, but when he realized that all the granaries of his kingdom, and perhaps of all the world, could not supply such an amount, he found it advisable to extricate himself from his predicament by having the poor inventor's head cut off.

The legend doesn't mention that the sovereign later paid an even higher price, becoming so enthralled by the new game that he lost his mind. The mythical inventor's greed, it turned out, was equaled only by that of the game itself.

Today's papers report the death of a man in a village not far from Vienna. Yesterday, Sunday morning, one Dieter Frisch succumbed to a gunshot wound. The medical examiner's report sets the time of death at 4 a.m., the result of a pistol shot fired at very close range, the bullet piercing the palate and exiting through the occipital lobe.

The newspaper accounts are accompanied by a recent photo of the deceased, shown relaxing in the grounds of his villa like a country squire just back from his daily walk. Dressed in light-colored linen, lounging in a wicker chair, he seems to be extending a hand to pet one of the two dogs huddled at his feet. I look at that picture and find it hard to recognize the face, shadowed as it is by the brim of what looks like a light-weight Panama hat. Is a man's physiognomy no more than an assemblage of mass and weight, the contours of a muscular structure? Or is there something more enduring, lying unchanged beneath the relentless layerings of time? Can it be that the person I knew lurks hidden beneath that name and that countenance? Only after a few moments' concentration do the features stored deep in my memory reemerge, like a transparency superimposed over that face eroded by age yet somehow still stubbornly youthful.

The headlines make much of the passing of this "eminent personality," but say nothing about how it actually happened. Under pressure from the family, staunchly opposed to the hypothesis of suicide, nearly all the papers speak of an "accident," "mishap," or death in "mysterious circumstances." Whatever the evidence may be, it becomes worthless in the absence of a plausible motive. Everyone who knew him seems prepared to swear that he had absolutely no reason to take his own life. He had never been depressed or listless. His latest checkup, a recent one, gave him a clean bill of health, and he was in enviable shape: at the age of sixty-eight still active in his favorite sports, tennis and horseback riding, despite a slight limp ever since an operation after an injury caused by a fall from a horse. Nor was there any hint of financial trouble. In fact, a few days ago he won a multimillion-dollar construction contract from the Bundesbank.

Frisch was one of those people upon whom fate seems to smile in every domain. He married a rich heiress and had four sons, all of whom now hold prominent social positions. He led a well-ordered, quiet life, spending four days a week in Munich managing his own business and returning on Friday to Vienna, to be driven to the place where he liked to spend all his free time: a villa ringed by a vast park in turn surrounded by a 125-acre game preserve. The property, built late in the eighteenth century, has long been a tourist attraction, open to the public in summer. Visitors are allowed to view the stud farm and stroll through the grounds, a true masterpiece of gardening and water management designed more than a century ago. The highlight is a concentric maze of ten-foot-high hedges leading to a chessboard-shaped clearing paved with squares of white and black marble. On opposite sides of the board, chess pieces have been painstakingly sculpted by pruning thick shrubs as tall as a man. The black pieces are of yew, the white of boxwood.

Like most people his age, Frisch was a creature of habit. On his three days a week in the villa he awoke promptly at seven-thirty and spent exactly five minutes in an indoor cold-water pool, followed by some calisthenics and a ritually meticulous toilet. At about eight o'clock, properly dressed, he would descend to the spacious sitting room for a frugal breakfast served on fine china: a cup of unsweetened black coffee and some whole-grain toast with a touch of marmalade. He would then withdraw to his study to spend the rest of the morning on his great passion, chess. He owned everything that had ever been written on the subject and boasted a precious collection of antique sets. Though he had not competed for years, he still held a master's ranking and was the editor of an authoritative chess magazine.

All evidence suggests that nothing ever impinged on his routine until that last Friday night. His driver picked him up at the station in Vienna as usual. They exchanged only a few words on the way back to the villa, where they arrived in the middle of the night—at a quarter to one to be exact. (The driver was always careful to time the trip.) Frisch got out of the car and, as always, went first to the dogs' compound, where he petted each of his "puppies," soothing their enthusiastic welcome. He then went into the house. Just as on every Friday.

But as early as Saturday morning his elderly housemaid noticed something strange in her master's behavior. Frisch looked as though he had slept little and badly. In fact, the woman was ready to swear that if he went to bed at all, he had not even undressed. Accustomed as she was to a clockwork household routine from which she herself took the greatest solace, she was alarmed by this sudden change in the master's habits.

Devoted servant that she was, however, she felt it was not her place to say anything to anyone, not even the other members of the staff. Nor did she inform Frisch's wife, partly because the couple occupied different wings of the villa and led what were effectively separate lives, appearing together only at rare official functions. According to the housemaid's account, Dr. Frisch ate no breakfast that morning, and his lunch, served at the usual hour, was returned untouched on the tray.

He seems to have spent the whole day alone in the house, receiving no visitors. Only when our witness came to serve him dinner in his study did she notice that a lamp had been turned on. It was still on when she fell asleep, at about two in the morning.

Well after eight o'clock on Sunday morning there was still no sign of Frisch. Concerned about the unusual delay, the maid went upstairs to the bedroom. Finding it empty and the bed not slept in, she thought at first that the master had spent the night elsewhere, though such was not his wont. She began to get suspicious when she saw that none of the cars was missing from the garage. She then knocked repeatedly at the study door, calling to him loudly. When she got no reply, she decided to go in, but found no one there. At that point she felt she had no choice but to wake Frisch's wife, a step not wholly without risk, since the lady of the house suffered from insomnia and was probably just then enjoying her first real repose.

The entire staff was soon mobilized to scour the twenty-eight rooms, the cellars, and the guest quarters, an unsuccessful search that was also extended to the grounds. Finally someone thought of bringing in the master's dogs. His two beloved German shepherds had been barking constantly all morning. When the first was turned loose, he darted straight for the garden labyrinth; the second, leashed, led them unhesitatingly to the spot. Frisch's body, supine in its own blood, lay in the center of the maze; his old army pistol was recovered a few feet away. The weapon was fitted with a silencer, and no one had heard the shot.

They looked in vain for a note, but all they found on his desk was a chess set in a complicated mid-game position.

It was a very strange board: light and dark patches of coarse cloth sewn together. Buttons of various sizes represented the pieces, symbols for each having been crudely scratched into the faces, apparently with a nail.

Of all the newspapers reporting the scene discovered by the first witnesses just one, a provincial sheet possibly short of firsthand information, commented on this apparently insignificant detail. Its article concluded: "No one will ever know why Dr. Frisch chose such a rag from his precious, renowned collection. Perhaps only to use it for his last match, with death."

None of the investigators suspected that the truth was shrouded in those vaguely melodramatic words. The strange chess pieces were of course dusted for prints, but removing them from the board obliterated what may have been the sole real clue—though I must admit it would have been hard to decipher.

Various scenarios have been suggested—suicide, accident, even the occasional whisper of crime—but no one has considered the possibility that Frisch's death was an execution, albeit deferred in space and time. Nor did anyone realize that his note was encoded in that chess position, and still less that it was addressed to the judge who had just sentenced him to die. No prints but the victim's were found on the pieces, but it was I who orchestrated the game. The chess set was mine, and I could reconstruct that position and play out all its variations blindfold. That defense, which Frisch had vainly tried to demolish from the summit of his prestigious magazine, was all that linked us to an evil nightmare of the past. That defense, which Frisch had the temerity to call the "Lüneburg variation," was the lead that enabled me to track him down.

Sentence was pronounced on Friday night, on the Munich–Vienna express.

As I said, every week Dieter Frisch went to his office in Munich for four days, leaving on Tuesday and returning to Vienna on the 7:20 express on Friday evening. He had been making the trip for years, and found the ride back especially welcome, since it afforded a few enjoyable hours of leisure. His usual companion was Mr. Baum, head of the Munich office, indispensable colleague, and friend since the bygone days of the war. They nearly always found a compartment all to themselves, and after drawing the curtains to discourage potential intruders, Mr. Baum would open his small traveling bag and take out a magnetized portable chess set. Thus began what had become the Friday night ritual. It made time pass in a flash. In fact, sometimes they couldn't even finish a game, since Mr. Baum got off one station before Frisch, who would spend the last forty-odd minutes alone, in pleasant contemplation of recent games.

Those who don't play chess may tend to think of it as a tedious game best suited to idle eccentrics and the elderly—people with vast patience and plenty of time to waste.

This is only partly true, for chess also requires uncommon energy and childlike mental vivacity. If players are sometimes portrayed as old men with furrowed brows, that is a merely symbolic depiction of an activity that consumes days, years, and even lifetimes in a single, unquenchable flame. Players relish the paradoxical compensation: time is forever frozen in a loop of the eternal present, while life away from the board comes to seem unbearably fast-paced. They therefore constantly seek to rediscover that state of grace, that nebulous yet limpid condition of dominion, that comes only from concentrating the mind on the game. Boredom? The chess player doesn't know the meaning of the word. Could a soldier on the attack feel even a flicker of boredom? In the whole history of chess only the great Capablanca must have felt something akin to it at the peak of his career, his play having become so perfect, and his confidence that he was unbeatable so unshakable, that he actually suggested modifying and enlarging the board, adding new pieces to make the game more challenging. But even he soon paid dearly for his sin of presumption.

10

Nearly everyone has sat at a board at one time or another, hefting the pieces, moving them back and forth along the squares, fascinated by the figures depicting a king, a queen, and a whole miniature army. Many have sampled the make-believe war, felt the thrill of victory and the humiliation of defeat. But only a few—call them chosen or cursed—have seen in these totemic sculptures a distant lineage from which they can never break free. Hans Mayer (my adopted son) and I are of that breed. I only hope that for Hans it is not too late, that in view of his youth he might yet emerge unscathed. I salute him for rededicating himself to painting and for leading a quiet life in which chess is no more than a pastime. But for me there is no escape, for I have little time left to live, and even death, I fear, will bring no release. Dieter Frisch, too, was part of this coterie. For many years he enjoyed complete security—new identity, new life, new career. It was his irresistible passion for chess that brought him down.

But let me go back a few days, to that Friday, a day that began so auspiciously for Frisch. His stays in Munich were a kind of vacation for him. He spent his nights with his lover in a cozy apartment on Ludwigstrasse that he'd bought for her a few years ago. Living with her forced him to alter his habits, though hardly against his will. Spartan mornings and frugal breakfasts gave way to lazy, somnolent nine o'clock awakenings followed by lavish Bavarian breakfasts, which for the most part he merely sampled. Only at around ten would he show up at the office, making an entrance like a lord visiting his fief, greeted by adoring vassals.

That morning he was awakened at eight-thirty by a phone

call from Mr. Baum reminding him that his presence was required for the signing of an important contract.

He bounded out of bed and got ready, humming in the bathroom as usual. Hilda, his lover, made the inevitable plentiful breakfast, which Frisch enjoyed more than usual. It was such a beautiful day, bathed by a radiant sunshine befitting late May, that he decided not to avail himself of the car that waited for him at the door, punctual as always. Instead he dismissed the driver and walked.

He spent the morning ironing out details of the contract, remaining in the office for a good part of the midday break. (He enjoyed showing his dependents that he was not afraid of work.) At around two he and Mr. Baum retired to their usual restaurant, where he not only allowed himself a stein of beer instead of the customary apple juice but also decided to linger after eating—another inhabitual act—nursing a glass of iced Obstler with his friend.

By the time he got back to the office it was almost four. He left word with his secretary that he did not want to be disturbed for any reason, then stretched out on the handsome, scented leather sofa in his presidential suite and dozed off.

He awoke at six-thirty—or rather, was awakened by the insistent buzzing of the intercom.

"Dr. Frisch," his secretary said, "please be advised that it is now six-thirty."

"Yes, all right," Frisch replied, clearly irritated at having been caught napping. "I know what time it is." In fact he would have been only too happy to stay asleep, and even as he spoke was not quite sure he was fully awake.

"One other thing . . ." the secretary ventured. "Someone was very insistent on speaking to you today. He phoned several times to say it was urgent that he see you."

"Who was it?"

"I don't know. He refused to give his name."

Frisch now realized that he wasn't dreaming. Having recovered from his moment of bewilderment, finding himself in his own clothes and his own familiar surroundings, he also recovered the full authority that was rightfully his.

"You know very well, Miss Hermes, that I grant no appointments on Friday, especially to someone who will not identify himself."

"Of course I know it," Miss Hermes replied, justifiably offended. She had worked for the firm for twenty-two years. "That's exactly why I felt bound to inform you."

"What are you trying to say?"

"Well," Miss Hermes replied, hesitating momentarily, "I had the impression he was trying to deceive me."

"Deceive you?"

"So it seemed. He claimed to be an old friend of yours. Or rather, he said he'd been 'sent' by an old friend."

"An old friend?"

"Precisely. But I fear this was only a means of acquiring information about your movements."

"About my movements?" Only now did it occur to Frisch that he was repeating his secretary's words, replacing periods with question marks. In the meantime his mind ran through a list of all the people, friend or foe, who might be lurking behind that phone call.

"How old was he?"

"How am I supposed to know that?" she answered, astonished. "I never laid eyes on him."

Frisch was close to losing patience. "From his voice, Miss Hermes, from his voice. I meant how old did he sound? Did he seem young? Old? Did he have an accent?"

Miss Hermes thought about it for a moment.

"Young, I'd say. And no accent."

Frisch sighed in relief. If he had anything to fear, it was only from the old, from people his own age, who shared a common past.

"What did you tell him?"

"Nothing . . . or nothing everyone doesn't already know," she stammered. Frisch felt as though he could see her, eyes wide behind her thick glasses, biting her lip. God knows how often he'd been tempted to get rid of her. If he hadn't already done so, it was only because of his unimpeachable discretion. But now . . .

"Meaning what, exactly?"

The secretary seemed on the verge of tears. "All I said was that you'd be leaving for Vienna this evening."

Though he had no idea why, Frisch was enraged by this admission, utterly unable to conceal his wrath. His words stung like a lash. "I can't tell you how disappointed I am, Miss Hermes. I never would have expected this from you."

"But I—"

Frisch let her say no more. He pushed the button to disconnect the intercom, deciding he would deal with her on his return to Munich.

He stood. He felt dizzy and nauseated. It was past six-thirty now. The light had waned, and it was almost dark in his office.

He went to the window and glanced down at the traffic eight stories below. The road was choked with cars. Throngs swarmed on the sidewalks in counterposed, intermingled streams. From so high up it all seemed fluid and impersonal, as though a mass of detritus were being swept away by water. That was all you really had to do to determine people's destiny: rise high enough to alter your view, making it divine. Compassion, mercy, love—these were relative, contingent terms, never absolute. What sort of love or compassion could you feel for a sacrificed chess piece? For a moment Frisch was struck by an irrepressible nostalgia for his youth. It suddenly occurred to him that all these people were wallowing in their own defeat. However splendid and lush things seemed, there was nevertheless a collective failure, to which the great majority seemed thoroughly resigned.

What could possibly rouse those somnambulant masses? Perhaps not even war.

The phone rang again. It was Baum, who seemed worried. "What's going on?" he asked. "The car's waiting."

Frisch shook himself out of his musings. "I'm on my way." But he lingered for a few more minutes, irritated by an itch no pleasant thought could scratch. That Hermes woman! That little busybody! Giving information to some stranger, probably a salesman or, worse, an insurance agent. Who else could it be? A friend? Could you have friends you didn't know about? Or maybe not a friend at all. Who the hell could it be? He had plenty of enemies, of course, but all were well known to him: competitors, politicians, a few women scorned, a jealous husband here and there. Who else? In his worst nightmares those enemies swelled to form a menacing horde. One of Frisch's recurrent anxieties was that he might fall victim to an ambush. It was a fear like a chronic migraine, now barely perceptible, now unbearable. Though he had never received threats of any kind, he feared assassins lurking along his habitual routes. Sometimes, when he stood at his window surveying the street below, he found himself wondering what his hypothetical executioner might look like. He would imagine picking him out among the crowd. One day it might be that man on the corner walking his dog; another, that motorcyclist garbed in black leather, the one who kept circling the block. Or today, perhaps, that student strolling along with his hands thrust deep in the pockets of his raincoat.

Frisch left the office, locked the door, and took the elevator to the underground garage. Baum was waiting for him in the car. Frisch sat down beside him in the backseat and nodded to the driver.

"Are you ill?" Baum asked.

"Not at all. Why?"

"You seem pale."

"I must have eaten too much." But Baum didn't seem convinced. "Oh, I almost forgot. Remind me about Miss Hermes when I get back. Something has to be done about her."

"Okay." Baum never questioned Frisch's decisions.

They rode in silence to the station. For the first time in the many years they'd known each other, Frisch felt physically repulsed by Baum. But he soon realized that this unpleasant sensation extended to all his surroundings, not least his own person.

At the bar in the station he downed a cognac, which seemed to revive him. The train stood waiting at the platform, fortunately with some compartments still vacant. They settled into the plush seats moments before the signal for departure was given, and only when he felt the train begin to move did it seem to Frisch that he'd fully recaptured his good humor. He gazed with renewed affability at Baum's thin face and customary gestures: removing and carefully folding the raincoat he always wore, pinching the creases of his trousers as he sat, placing his leather briefcase on his knees and opening it with simultaneous clicks of the side latches, and finally taking out the chess set so carefully it might have been a reliquary, putting it on the little fold-down table and meticulously setting up the pieces. His last act before starting the game was to rummage in his pants pocket for a one-pfennig coin, which he placed alongside the board. Frisch did likewise. Such were the symbolic stakes.

Baum was a decent player, no genius, but neither could he be called incompetent. His enviable technique compensated for his lack of talent. He was a good theorist, his openings always impeccable. True, he was short on ideas; whenever he tried to depart from beaten paths, he wound up outplayed, but on the whole he was a worthy opponent, never easily defeated. Usually they had time for two or even three games. They would run quickly through the opening, and after some skirmishing in the center and a few exchanges of pieces, would decide whether or not the game was worth continuing. Certain positions inevitably resulted in a draw. In that case they would start over, gradually selecting more risky variations. Baum, however, was always cautious, making only prudent, tested moves. Indeed, he was content to draw, considering that a good result. But sometimes they would find themselves immersed in a single, long game so satisfying that they would pause to examine it, analyzing all its variations.

One characteristic apparently common to all chess players is a refusal to admit that their position in a lost game was truly indefensible. So it was that Baum, when he lost, would obstinately review every move, seeking to discover where and when he went wrong. Their games and the subsequent analysis often afforded Frisch tasty morsels for his chess column.

Tonight Baum was playing white. The queen's pawn opening was his favorite. He liked to sail on still waters, aboard a solid craft. But Frisch didn't feel like running through the usual scenario. He decided to stir things up a bit. With Baum you could afford to court a risk or two.

"Let's see you get out of this, old man," Frisch said, rapidly making his opening move. But it soon became clear that his game plan was completely different from usual. He was dying to see good old Baum's face when he realized what variation he was going to have to deal with. Was Frisch's desire to involve himself in the complications of such a dangerous defense a joke? Or was it a kind of challenge to himself?

Chess players tend to have the same biased attitude toward the game as they do toward the world, with their own likes and dislikes, convictions and irritants. Frisch considered himself a purist with a horror of anything that wasn't logical and linear, or at least reducible to some established theory. His sound evaluation of forces was based more on the quantity of the pieces than on the quality of the game. He was, in sum, a man who couldn't stand to lose—and not only at chess; a man unable to renounce his own deep-rooted convictions, even a little.

18

It had been less than a year since he'd happened upon this variation for black in the course of his analyses for the magazine. It had cropped up in tournaments here and there, scoring incomprehensible success. It called at a certain point for a knight to be sacrificed in exchange for just two pawns, but this maneuver prevented white from securing the position of his king, thus initiating a threat to it. If white decided to maintain his material advantage, he had to resign himself to remaining in a defensive posture for a long time.

The variation had immediately struck Frisch as an affront to his own canons of aesthetic order, and he dealt with the matter fully in the pages of his magazine, seeking to demolish the variation, demonstrating just how thoroughly unfounded it was. His weighty study, serialized in several issues, was entitled "The Lüneburg Variation," which he described as "incoherent," "rash," and "quarrelsome." But sometimes we hate something so much that we wind up identifying with it, and Frisch was now making exactly the moves he deprecated. He must have felt a thrill of transgression in thus acting contrary to his own beliefs. In adopting his opponent's viewpoint, perhaps for the first time, he realized how different things could seem just by turning the board around.

He wondered whether Baum would even remember the variation.

But of course Baum had been an invaluable aide in the nerve-racking analyses of those games. And yes, he had noticed. And how!

"Oh," he exclaimed, obviously astonished, almost as if to say, *That* devil raising his head again!

Frisch pressed on. However meticulously he'd studied it,

there always seemed to be some aspect of the variation that eluded him. He wondered why he'd gone looking for this kind of trouble. He had a sudden urge to suggest that they abandon the game and start another, but he knew Baum would count an abandonment a victory, and he had no intention of conceding any such thing. At most he would grant him a draw now and then. The few times he'd happened to win, Baum boasted for weeks. And just as a single victory can redeem many a defeat, so a single defeat can devalue or even eradicate a long string of successes. But at bottom, Frisch was optimistic. If he played with the requisite attention, he could at least try to finish the game even.

Immersed as he was in his own thoughts, he didn't even notice that another passenger had entered the compartment and was about to take a seat beside them. It was rare that anyone would occupy *their* compartment in defiance of the drawn curtains. Frisch glanced up from the board and treated the intruder to a gaze laden with annoyance. He had a way of looking at people askance, a technique he retained from his army past. He never met anyone's eyes, but instead focused with a kind of disapproval on a point on his interlocutor's throat, as though detecting a stain on his collar, or an insignia that had come unsewn.

Feeling himself observed, the young man said something under his breath, murmured a greeting, and sat down.

The intruder might have been a little over twenty. He had blondish shoulder-length hair, he needed a shave, and he was wrapped in a raincoat that was white but no longer spotless, buttoned to the neck. It was a style of dress that Frisch quite naturally detested.

The boy slumped low in his seat and kept his hands deep in his pockets. He carried a flat leather briefcase on a shoulder strap. That he had no other baggage gave Frisch hope that he was making only a short trip.

After watching them for a few minutes, the boy opened his briefcase, took out some drawing paper, and cleared his throat to attract their attention. "With your permission, gentlemen," he said, "I would like to make you a sketch of yourselves playing chess."

Frisch curtly refused, and the boy, apparently resigned, seemed to settle back into his seat. He slipped the briefcase off his shoulder and placed it beside him, first extracting from it a small packet of gray cloth, which he hurriedly tucked into the pocket of his raincoat.

Frisch returned to his own thoughts, but the alien presence disturbed him. He cast rapid occasional glances at the stranger, who never took his eyes from the board. The nearly imperceptible shifts of his pupils suggested that he was assessing various possibilities. Baum, too, was wholly absorbed in the game. Finding himself in a favorable position, he concentrated with his full attention, moving his pieces with an evident air of satisfaction.

They played for another half hour, at which point Frisch offered a draw, convinced that Baum, as usual, would accept. But to his great disappointment, his opponent balked, pursing his lips as though savoring a vintage wine and finally declining with effrontery: "I'd rather see how it comes out, if you don't mind."

After which, move upon move, Frisch came to realize that despite his best efforts he was heading for an untenable endgame, a course he knew well, having analyzed it thoroughly, though his had been a biased analysis. Convinced as he was that the "Lüneburg variation" could not hold up, he sought, perhaps unconsciously, to bolster his conviction. As checkmate drew near, he turned over his king in resignation.

"Q.E.D., my dear Baum," he exclaimed with feigned self-assurance, though unable to conceal the sullen expression typically assumed by those unwilling to lose when they actually do. "This variation doesn't hold up." And inasmuch as defeat always makes us indulgent, he turned to the young spectator almost as if seeking to involve him. The youth continued to stare at the board with a doubtful expression, as though adding up accounts that didn't balance. But there was no way to tell how well he knew the game.

The young man cleared his throat and said, "It doesn't seem to me that you made the best possible moves."

Frisch was dumbfounded. It took effort to absorb the affront, but after recovering his poise—for only with the greatest of poise can one reply to an incompetent—he smirked.

"You think not?"

If there was anything he couldn't bear, it was an opinion issued by an amateur spectator who perhaps barely knew how the pieces moved. The conductor, for instance, was just such a specimen, his arrival an inescapable irritant. His view of chess was shortsighted and blinkered. He was the sort who saw checkmates looming everywhere like desert mirages, and it was often necessary to keep his hand from falling upon the board, bringing disaster in its wake. But while the conductor was a constant if predictable threat, this dilettante's intrusion was entirely unforeseeable, even unprecedented. In the many years Frisch and Baum had been making this trip, there had been a few occasions when an interloper who could have chosen a vacant compartment instead decided to inflict himself on them, feeling free to ramble on endlessly. Harmless, superficial comments by incompetents were of course readily confuted. But this intruder seemed to know the game, and he'd spoken with a clear intent to provoke.

Frisch managed to calm himself. It even occurred to him that this fine young gentleman might be a source of some amusement.

"What makes you think there were any better moves in this position?" he asked, leaning forward slightly from the waist.

The young man grinned pointedly, almost scornfully. "In this position, clearly not," he said.

"Meaning?"

"Meaning that we'd have to back up a few moves for me to explain it to you."

Frisch fought another brief battle with himself. "Really."

"Really. This variation has to be played as dynamically as possible, not reduced to the defensive immobility you imposed. Its aim is to queen a pawn—that's the essential threat. Without some compensation for the initial knight sacrifice, you face a losing endgame, that's obvious."

"Obvious," Baum muttered to himself, not taking his eyes from the board. "Obvious," he repeated, as if gripped by a mild seizure of echolalia.

Frisch was about to say something when the young man held up a hand.

"I've played this variation more times than I can count," he said. "In fact, I *always* play it against the queen's pawn opening."

"Successfully, I presume," Frisch remarked, sarcastically.

"Oh yes," the young man replied. "Eighty percent of the time. Which with black is true success."

"My dear sir," Frisch announced, no longer able to contain himself, "I have but one thing to say to you: this defense is worthless. It had a sudden spurt of popularity about a year ago, primarily as a passing fad (for even in chess, fashions come and go), until I myself felt obliged to demolish it in my magazine." He spoke with authority. "Its sole—and I repeat, its *sole*—advantage is that he who troubles the waters sometimes creates unsightly turbulence in which an opponent may slip and fall. But nothing more. It relies on surprise alone. It's based on trickery, certainly not intelligence." Here he fell silent, apparently regretting his vehemence. Settling on a more neutral tone, speaking with the care with which he might select a sober tie to match an afternoon suit, he added, "In any event, it seems you play chess, too."

"Not anymore," the young man replied.

"You seem to keep up, though."

"I played for years, until I got my master's rating. But it's been a while since I've had anything to do with chess."

"Well," Frisch suggested magnanimously, "why not seize the opportunity?" The intruder's arrival had been annoying, but now that Frisch realized he was dealing with an expert, he suddenly changed his mind. "If you wish . . ." he went on, gesturing broadly at the tiny chessboard at which Mr. Baum was still staring, as though transfixed by his victorious position.

The young man coyly declined. "I couldn't, I really couldn't."

"But why not? What better occasion could there be? I am Dr. Frisch, master and international chess referee. Also editor of the magazine *Der Turm*."

The young man shook the hand that was offered him, nodding briefly and muttering, "Mayer."

Frisch refused to give up. "You can play white, if you wish. Or take black, and use this variation."

The young man shook his head resolutely. "I'm sorry to seem discourteous. I said 'couldn't,' but the truth is, I'm *unable* to play against an opponent."

At that even Baum shook himself out of his torpor and looked curiously at the young man—Mayer was his name, yes? or so Baum thought he'd said—who now seemed to feel dutybound to explain his refusal.

"It's a question of nerves, I suppose. I mean, I think I'm still a good player. It's just that I don't have the heart to play against a flesh-and-blood person."

"The heart?" Frisch asked, flabbergasted. "You don't have the heart?"

"It's beyond my control," the young man went on. "Probably a phobia, but I just can't help it. Chess nearly ruined my life. It brought me to the edge of insanity. Overnight I lost everything, I had nothing left. Even now it's hard to believe how it happened. I wound up homeless, spending nights on the street or in public shelters. There were times I truly thought I was mad. In one place where I had to stay for a while, with the dregs of the city, there was a man who claimed he could figure out what had gone wrong in someone's brain. He gave me forms to fill out and asked very embarrassing questions. He was determined to find out why I'd fallen into that state. He wanted to put his finger on exactly what had robbed me of my will to live. When I explained the problem to him, he seemed very interested. In fact, he was the only one who ever listened to what I had to say and believed my story. He concluded that the reason I couldn't play chess anymore was that I saw my opponent as a father figure with whom I was in conflict. And his diagnosis was right on the mark, albeit based on mistaken premises. It wasn't my real father, you see, and the story I told him certainly wasn't a figment of my imagination or a product of my unconscious need to punish myself for some misdeed, as he claimed. Though I admit that at the time I was beginning to have doubts about that myself.

"It all started with my passion for chess, a game into which I was initiated in a most unusual way . . ."

Finally the young man's words seemed to capture the attention of his audience. For the first time Frisch raised his pale blue gaze to Mayer's eyes, revealing a more clement countenance, or so it seemed to Mayer. And this, indeed, was exactly what the boy'd been waiting for, fearing it would never come, as one sometimes seeks human responses in the eyes of trained animals. Frisch's features suddenly relaxed. He abandoned his initial reserve, though inadvertently rather than with genuine intent.

Mayer sighed deeply. He seemed less tense. The veil of hoarseness that had betrayed his nervousness now vanished from his voice.

He squeezed the cloth packet buried in the pocket of his raincoat as if to reassure himself he hadn't forgotten why he was on this train. He could now regard his adversary without fear. Despite everything he knew about him, he saw him as ordinary and defenseless, a man who—having let the mask of rigidity drop for an instant—truly looked his age, a man nearly old, his iron-gray hair cut short to conceal his spreading baldness, his body healthy and well nourished, cared for with devotion, doubtless throbbing with gratitude beneath its dark and perfectly tailored suit.

The other man, Baum, was clearly quite commonplace. He was sitting with his legs crossed, turned three-quarters toward Mayer, hands on one knee, fingers interlaced, seemingly engrossed in his own thoughts, but only so as to be able to listen without appearing to.

The train passed an ironworks that cast blinding flashes against the windowpanes. A village glided by, its lights whirling, leaving pylons and bright patches of blue in its wake, until finally the black rumble of the forest returned.

The two men's silence, along with Frisch's openly aroused and attentive curiosity, now persuaded Mayer to begin his tale.

It was as a child that I became fascinated with chess. I learned the first moves from my father, who was a talented amateur. In fact, one of my most vivid memories of him is of how he looked as he leaned over the board deep in thought.

But both my parents were killed in an automobile accident when I was six. I was sent to live with my maternal grandmother in Vienna.

For years I thought no more about chess, which remained a dim, mysterious memory linked to the magic world of my early childhood. My father's chess set lay in a drawer in my grandmother's house. It was one of those boards that closed into a case containing the boxwood and ebony pieces. But board and pieces languished unattended in that drawer, along with other objects that had belonged to him: his metal tobacco case, a few pipes, a razor with a tortoiseshell handle. No more than keepsakes to hold on to.

I was about thirteen when chess took possession of me again, and it happened in a very strange way, almost as if the game's dual essence were revealed to me in a sign.

One spring morning I was sitting with my grandmother at an outdoor café downtown, watching the remains of my ice cream melt in the glass cup. Suddenly bloodstains dotted the gleaming marble tabletop. My grandmother leaped to her feet, trying to stanch the flow of blood from my nose with a napkin. The woman who owned the café, after washing me off with tap water, brought me to an elegant back room whose walls were entirely mirrored. I was told to sit absolutely still until the nosebleed stopped. After reminding me not to move, my grandmother left me alone. But as it turned out, I was not entirely alone, for all at once I heard murmurs from behind a thick red velvet curtain that divided the room in two. It was as though someone was trying to talk without making noise, and the boredom of enforced immobility made me especially curious to find out who it was. My head was tilted back; I was holding ice to my forehead, staring at a point directly above me, and I noticed that if I cast my eye toward the far end of the room, the reflection on the ceiling, also mirrored, allowed me to see what was happening beyond the curtain, backstage, so to speak. Soon I recognized something familiar: a chessboard, ringed by people who, judging by the widespread baldness and graying hair, seemed to be quite elderly. They were staring at the gleaming quadrangle as though awaiting an oracle's reply. But there was something else as well, something I was unable to bring into focus no matter how I tried. It was in stark contrast to the room's solemnity, and though I was unable to reconcile it with the stooped shoulders and bent heads, it somehow brought a joyful image to mind, as though all those people were waiting for a punch line.

"If you're all better, we can go," I heard my grandmother say.

But instead I stood and crossed the room to the curtain as if moving from one dream to another. Perhaps my grandmother was too taken aback to stop me, or perhaps she was intimidated by the pervasive silence and didn't dare raise her voice. In any case, she merely lifted an arm in a gesture of surprise that I barely noticed, for I had already stepped beyond the curtain and approached the knot of people crowded around the table. No one paid attention to me, even when I elbowed my way through to see the board. Once I did, I understood the reason for the strange feeling I'd just had. Two people were seated at the table: one, with his back to me, was an old man with a full head of white hair and dressed in dark clothing. Opposite him was a skinny, blond child who seemed to be about my age. Motionless at the board, ringed by all those men so much older than him, he looked like the boy Jesus being questioned by the doctors in the temple.

It was the old man's move, and soon he raised a hand, lifted a piece, and placed it elsewhere on the board with an air of extreme dejection. The child sitting opposite immediately followed suit, saying nothing, but acting with such merciless and mocking confidence as to suggest that this was the climactic move.

I'd always thought you had to announce your victory by saying "mate" or "checkmate," even if only for your own satisfaction. But to my surprise, nothing of the kind happened here. The old man thought for another few minutes—or rather, it seemed as though he were attentively assessing a precious object or evaluating the authenticity of a work of art—after which he merely stood and shook his opponent's hand.

Suddenly all the people who till then had been holding their breath began to chatter loudly, dozens of hands falling upon the board in terrible confusion. At that moment my grandmother took me by the arm and began to lead me away. I didn't want to go. I began to kick and protest, but Grandmother was implacable. As she dragged me away, clearing a path among the people who continued to clamor around the board, I turned for a last look and saw—not a shadow of doubt about it—that what I had taken for a child was in fact an adult, a dwarf with a slight, well-proportioned body and a childish face, hairless and wrinkled. It also seemed that he looked at me as if winking in complicity.

Was that the day of my initiation? I'm not sure. But I do know that from then on, my interest in chess was gradually reawakened. I was a pail being filled a drop at a time. The first thing I did was to rummage through the objects that had belonged to my father, taking out the chess set as though digging up buried treasure. I counted the pieces, turning them over in my fingers as if seeing them for the first time and then setting them up on the board as my father had taught me years ago. It seemed to me I could sense within myself all the emotions embodied in those quintessential sculptures. It was like being present at the reading of a will naming me as sole heir.

The passion was immediate and relentless. For a while I merely moved the pieces around the board, feeling their consistency and simply looking at them. They were my first thought in the morning and my last at night. They appeared in all my dreams. I had yet to play a single game, but I pictured myself as an unbeatable champion. When anyone asked me what I wanted to be when I grew up, I never had the slightest doubt.

Apart from the set, my father had also left me quite a few chess books, which I flipped through, with a kind of avid superficiality, trying not to drown in their seas of abstruse symbols.

Then one day I decided the time had to come to put my presumed mastery to the test. Finding opponents wasn't easy. Whenever we come to feel true passion for something, we also realize with dismay that the world that seems so all-consuming to us is little appreciated by others, even unknown. I had no one to play with apart from my classmates, with whom I sometimes managed a few quick games, and I was so eager for potential opponents that all I ever wanted to know about anyone I met was whether he played chess. I had no interest in anyone who said no, while those who acknowledged having even the barest knowledge of the rules rose immediately in my estimation, only to become my victims once they agreed to test themselves against me.

So my first opponents were friends and classmates. But not even my grandmother was spared. Often she sought to elude me by dragooning some unfortunate family friend who'd happened by.

Like any beginner, I preferred practice to theory and play to study, believing the latter superfluous in the presence of the omniscient genius who dwelt within me, sometimes suggesting the winning move.

You know, of course, that Alekhine considered chess an art while Capablanca saw it as pure craft. Lasker, on the other hand, thought of it as combat. I saw it not as combat but as a cockfight, with much squawking and feathers flying everywhere. I paid little heed to defense, sacrificing pieces without a second thought, content to tame small fires while failing to notice that the entire edifice might be ablaze. I was convinced that imagination (which I was sure I possessed in abundance) would always get the better of the wretched bookkeepers' calculations favored by so many of my opponents, who, with their meticulous balance sheets of gains and losses, finished with the extra pawn that guaranteed victory. I dreamed of playing like the great Morphy or the "immortal" and "evergreen" Anderssen, mounting a series of ever gaudier sacrifices concluding with a checkmate with the sole piece remaining to me, executed like the touch of a foil. But talent is not always commensurate with passion, and so it was that I clung stubbornly to a dream I could never fulfill. The reality was that I was leagues from understanding the game. The passion grew within me nevertheless, reaching abnormal proportions.

At seventeen I enrolled in the Academy of Fine Arts, moving out of my grandmother's house and into student lodgings. My grandmother was no weepy white-haired old lady but, on the contrary, a charming woman of fifty-five, an ex-singer still courted by devoted admirers, who led a glittering, not to say dissolute, life and was clearly relieved no longer to be saddled with a boy who persisted in calling her grandmother, though of course I don't mean to say she didn't love me.

I shared a room with another student, who had absolutely no interest in chess. I, however, was now devoted to it exclusively, and thought of nothing else. It might well be said that I ate, drank, and breathed chess. If Plato maintained that God was a geometer, for me there was a god who played chess eternally.

Evenings I would wander the streets of old Vienna peering into the windows of crowded coffeehouses in search of a game, invariably attracted to places where I saw people gathered around tables but almost always disappointed to find that the spectators were watching card players—a species that seemed enormously widespread. Rarely was I lucky enough to spy a chessboard among the card tables, overseen, more than inhabited, by fossilized players who, judging by their ages and the time they took to move, appeared to be continuing games begun in their youth, like the two players in the famous joke who—first as adolescents, then as adults, and finally as old men—sit staring at the same position until one finally asks the other, "Whose move is it?"

Then one evening my wish was granted. Turning into a dimly lit, unknown street where nothing stirred, I suddenly saw a sign depicting a red angel clutching a black lily. It was a beer hall called Der Rote Engel, and I could hardly believe my eyes when I glanced through the smoke-darkened windows: not one but dozens of boards, and onlookers gathered around the small tables as feverish as though watching cockfights.

I had stumbled inadvertently into my own world, one whose existence I'd never suspected. I had always pictured chess clubs as exclusive institutions located in inaccessible reaches, like Masonic lodges, admittance to which required a ritual trial. But here I had only to step across the threshold to find myself in one of the city's chess clubs—not the most renowned, but probably the most varied, and surely the noisiest.

I began attending religiously, but since no one seemed to notice me, I had no choice but to join the so-called kibitzers who hovered over the tables lavishing shrill advice upon the players, most of it disastrous. At the Rote Engel, chess was not a discipline but a demential amusement in which all the rules of the game were bent. Onlookers and participants guffawed sarcastically amid cigar smoke and beer steins, often hurling insults and even fists. I soon realized that the club was split into two distinct sections. The good-timers occupied the area around the bar, where it didn't take long to get served. Sometimes they merged with the card players, partly because they, too, played for money. The others, more serious and restrained, withdrew to the back of the room, the quietest part of the premises, where they spent the evening feeding little more than their gray matter. Relations between the two factions were not always the best. It was like an eternal struggle between aristocrats and plebeians, accounts being settled at an annual tournament in which all club members had to participate.

My first opponent was a rather odd old man with an alcoholic's face. He was a ragpicker by trade and was himself dressed in rags, though apparently the cream of his wares, patched but of good material. His shoes were worn down at the heels but free from holes.

He would arrive towing a wooden pushcart crammed with

rags and covered with a waxed tarp to shield the merchandise from bad weather. After pulling the cart into a little courtyard behind the beer hall and securing one wheel with a chain and padlock, he would stride boldly in, greeting everyone loudly. Most of the time everyone ignored him and even tried to avoid him, but he never seemed to care. He would take a seat at a table and set up the pieces with great optimism, as though laying out a sales display and waiting for a potential customer.

For some time I tried to keep away from him. I could tell by the way he looked at me that he had great hopes for me, but if no one else wanted to play with him, why should I? Then one evening, against my better judgment, I accepted an explicit invitation. For a novice like myself it would have been better to watch other people's games.

I soon realized why no one wanted to play with him. He had all the worst habits of a coffeehouse player. Not only did he ponder his moves interminably, but when he realized he'd made a mistake, he thought nothing of taking his piece back, with great nonchalance, and it was therefore almost impossible to enjoy the satisfaction of beating him. On top of that, he commented on the game in outlandish, incomprehensible phrases that sounded like medieval student slang.

"Deo gratias . . . kakkus!" he'd exclaim when he managed to check an opponent's king. Immersed in his gloomy reflections, he would mumble his nonsense words, which seemed to have an invigorating effect on him, like drum rolls on soldiers in a pitched battle. *"Du, du, Strumpfel Lump . . ."* he'd repeat in an unending refrain.

That phrase was his nickname, and I, too, came to call him Strumpfel Lump. He played no better than I did, but I found his psalmody soporific, and he had some experience, which came to his rescue in difficult moments. Not infrequently he turned a desperate position in his favor by exploiting my youthful impetuosity. But he didn't show up every evening. When he was absent, I had no choice but to be a spectator.

It didn't take me long to sort out all or most of the denizens of the Red Angel. Among them was the man who was to become my master. His name was Tabori, and he was perhaps the only club member accepted and esteemed by both factions.

I would have liked to learn more about him, but Strumpfel Lump was of little help. A stein of beer went a long way toward loosening the old man's tongue, and once I managed to decipher what he was raving about in his rare moments of loquacity, I learned quite a lot about the picturesque personalities who frequented the Rote Engel, but he never said a word about Tabori, even though I was sure they knew each other. When they met, they exchanged glances that lingered the little extra that suggests a greeting, and once, when the old man raised a glass too many and began to annoy the people around him, I had the clear feeling that after countless unsuccessful attempts to calm him down, a single look from Tabori drove him out with his tail between his legs. So one day I treated him to three steins and summoned the courage to venture a direct question.

"What about Tabori?" I asked.

Strumpfel Lump roused himself from his ramblings. His inexpressive eyes seemed to come suddenly into focus, as when a man pulls his trousers up. For the first time ever he met my eyes.

"Stay away from that man," he declared, frowning like a country preacher. "That man . . . that man has played in hell."

That was all he would say, and it only sharpened my curiosity.

■   ■   ■

Tabori was a stout man who looked about sixty but could have been much older. His face was shadowed by stubble, but his hands were well tended, and he dressed with some affectation. He carried a walking stick, which lent him an air of slightly dated refinement. He'd arrive at exactly six-thirty and begin to wander among the tables. When he approached a board, even the most impassioned players fell silent, trying to think for as long as he lingered in the vicinity. Rumor had it that he'd been a great player in his youth, that he'd played against champions, even holding the unbeatable Capablanca to a draw. But I never saw him play a single game. All he did was watch, strolling among the tables like the head of a clinic on daily rounds, issuing a comment here, a prognosis there, many prescriptions, and a rare word of comfort. Now and then he stood longer than usual at a board, staring with an almost painful intensity.

One day as he was reviewing the boards he was kind enough to stop at mine. I was playing Strumpfel Lump, whose chanted laments ceased when Tabori came near. We were at a critical point in the game. It was my move, and I was having trouble deciding. I had a choice between a brilliant continuation not all of whose consequences were predictable and a modest pawn advance that would consolidate my position. Though I faced myriad threats from my opponent, I was confident I had the situation well in hand, and since Tabori was looking over my shoulder, I rashly opted for what I considered the more brilliant sequence. When I picked up the piece I meant to move, Tabori turned and walked away even before I replaced it on the board. It soon became clear that my attack was premature.

I didn't sleep a wink that night, tormented by the thought

that Tabori had witnessed my error. His sudden departure burned in my mind like a scornful reproach. I was so upset I no longer had the heart to play in his presence.

By that time he was the person I most admired in the world. He'd contended with the greatest living players, holding his own against them. For a beginner like myself he was a model. Had I been capable of it, I would have imitated his gait and his voice.

As I said, these were early days, the most beautiful phase of any endeavor, when everything seems like a dream. At the time I had no idea of the price art must pay to life, the odious tribute the ideal owes to the material.

I've seen the most amazing tricks performed by trained animals who bear the indelible marks of countless tortures beneath their elegance of movement. All pleasure seems to vanish once perfection is attained—indeed, long before it. But I never imagined that Tabori himself would be the man to reveal the game's dark side to me. As I said, I was still immersed in the dream, and every evening it took human form in that man's shape. From the moment I entered the Rote Engel I would keep watch on the door through which Tabori would enter, punctual as ever. Only then did I awaken to my surroundings, which seemed purified by his presence. I would follow him without his noticing—or so I believed—not leaving him alone for an instant. I carefully examined the games he lingered over and was sometimes lucky enough to hear his comments as they ended. Often he reconstructed a position he found interesting, going back ten or fifteen moves, demonstrating an intricate branching of winning solutions. He had a curious manner of removing pieces from the board, holding them between the fingers of one hand and replacing them in the same order so quickly and accurately that his gestures seemed like a magician's sleight of hand. To hear him tell it, everything was always crystal clear.

My curiosity about this man grew so sharp that I began following him when he left, at first for a few hundred yards, later for longer, but it was hard: he never took the same route twice and often stopped or turned to retrace his steps. Lurking against walls, I would stalk him through the alleyways of the old city, but no matter how careful I was, he always eluded me in the end, until one evening the hunter became the prey. I was on my way home, having lost him as usual, when suddenly I had the feeling someone was tracking me. The feeling grew sharper with each step, until finally I realized I was being shadowed by two individuals who kept well behind me, slowing when I did, speeding up when I tried to lose them. At one point I turned a corner, planning to break into a full run the moment I was out of sight, but just then I saw someone in the distance coming toward me. I felt lost. I wasn't sure why, but there was something ghostly and frightening about the indistinct shape, something that made me want to turn back to face the two men behind me rather than go forward to meet it. The closer it came, the harder it was to believe my own eyes. I told myself it couldn't be true, but when he passed beneath a streetlamp and I saw that he was grinning, I realized he'd figured out I'd been following him and had cut off my retreat, through what witchcraft I have no idea. Since there was no point in trying to hide or slip away, I stepped out of the shadows.

"Humid tonight, don't you think?" Tabori calmly observed. "What are you doing here, boy?"

I was across the street from him, just a few yards away. The two men stood in a doorway about thirty paces behind me. Confused as I was, I heard myself lying, telling him I lived in the neighborhood. He smiled. I'm sure he knew it wasn't true. Was it merely my impression, or was there a threat behind the smile?

"You've been following me for some time now," he said. "Is there anything I can do for you?"

Had the accusation not been followed by the question, which admittedly sounded purely rhetorical, I'd have beaten a retreat and eventually forgotten about Tabori and chess forever. But at that moment, emboldened by a sudden surge of temerity, I uttered the request I'd long harbored. "Master," I said—the word containing the echo of every voice that had ever spoken it from time immemorial—"I would like you to teach me to play chess."

He seemed genuinely surprised. "That's why you've been following me?" he said, as if to himself.

I nodded eagerly. My heart was in my throat, and I had no breath to utter even a single syllable.

Tabori smiled sadly and, I thought, with a kind of compassion. Menace vanished from his expression. He made a rapid, barely perceptible gesture, and the two men in the doorway walked away.

Suddenly he seemed uneasy, as if ashamed of himself for having been so suspicious of me, perhaps assuming I wanted to rob him or stab him in the back. But I couldn't understand what he'd been afraid of.

"In other words, you'd *really* like to play chess?"

"Yes," I insisted.

He chuckled. It was the first time I'd ever heard him laugh, and it was not a sneer of disdain—as I feared at first—but an expression of satisfaction, the satisfaction of a hunter who finally has his prey after stalking it for so long. It was a brief laugh that seemed like mere illusion once it faded.

I don't know how long we stood silent and motionless in that alleyway. Tabori seemed to be weighing my request, and finally he shook his head. "I don't know, I just don't know. I don't know if I can do it. A lot will depend on you, on whether your desire is real."

"It is," I said.

"Or whether you're ready for the sacrifices that—"

"Anything you ask of me."

He nodded at my impassioned profession of faith, patted me on the back, and walked away.

You can imagine how anxiously I awaited his reply. Of course, I stopped following him at the club. In fact, I acted as if I didn't even know him. I didn't want to be importunate. Nearly a month went by, and one evening, as I was beginning to lose hope, he approached me and handed me a little card with an address and a phrase written in ink: "Sunday morning at ten."

I kept the appointment after a torturous wait and a sleepless night.

It was autumn, and a thick, fine rain was falling. I arrived a good half hour early and roamed the neighborhood to kill time. The address on the card was a dilapidated five-story apartment building. Things always turn out different from what we imagine. Never would I have expected such a place. The building looked like the sole survivor of an implacable urban renewal that stripped everything around it bare, leaving it standing like the last slice of cake on a plate—which was just what it looked like, a thin wedge dividing the street into two lanes that hugged its sides. The only entrance was through a hotel, the Fischer Pension, according to its crumbling sign. The rest of the façade was covered by the remnants of the shutters of what must have been flourishing enterprises in times long past: a bookseller, a pharmacy, a tailor's shop. But these places, once full of life, had fallen into the oblivion of dust and ruin. The only one still displaying merchandise was a junk shop whose window bore dark letters spelling out the name Tabori.

As I waited for ten o'clock I tried in vain to peer through the window to the darkest recesses, searching for some precious chessboard among all that detritus. When your mind is ruled by passion, you want the entire world to offer signs and symbols. But to my great disappointment all I saw was worthless objects piled one atop the other: chests of drawers of all shapes and sizes scattered at random on the shop floor, holy-water stoups and prie-dieus and heaps of bronze crucifixes and candelabra with seven branches—like booty abandoned by a horde of idol smashers.

It began to rain harder. I walked around the building seeking other entrances, but found none. The rear wall was buttressed by iron scaffolding as though it were in danger of falling. It looked like a gigantic stage set. Finally I decided to ring the bell of the hotel, since its number was the one on the card. I pressed hard and heard a faint tinkle inside, but the door stayed stubbornly closed. I tried repeatedly, knocking loudly as well, and finally, after what seemed a very long time, a window was laboriously pulled open on the floor above and an elderly and completely bald man leaned out to tell me curtly that the hotel was closed for repairs.

"I'm looking for Tabori," I shouted. "He gave me this address."

The man seemed not to understand. "It's closed," he repeated. After I'd told him for the nth time with all the breath I could muster that I was looking for Tabori, even waving the card, now sodden in the rain, he closed the window and left me standing in the downpour. Exasperated, I rang the bell again. I kicked and pounded at the door. Finally I heard the footsteps of someone who seemed to be wearing heavy wooden clogs. The door opened.

"There's no need for all that racket," snarled the same man who'd opened the window, the reproach assuming unusual gravity, coming as it did from someone so obviously hard of hearing.

He showed me in, closed the door behind me, and threw the bolt. I stood dripping wet in what had once been the lobby of a hotel. It surely hadn't seen a guest in decades, yet everything was still in place, from the thick registration books on the counter to the numbered keys hanging neatly from a wooden rack. In one pigeonhole there were even yellowed letters no one had ever bothered to pick up. The reception room contained a few shabby armchairs that stood around a low table bearing a plastic ashtray bisected by a cigar butt. The only signs of life were an old raincoat hanging from a coat rack and an unusually elegant item in the umbrella holder: a malacca walking stick whose brass handle was a greyhound's head.

The man didn't give me much time to look around. He motioned me to follow him. I was very surprised to see that he was wearing a striped room-service apron, as anachronistic as a medieval costume amid all that desolation.

We walked to the back of what must once have been a dining room and was now a storage space for chairs and tables piled almost to the ceiling. We stopped at a small service elevator with a wrought-iron door. He motioned me to go in, and after enclosing me in the tiny cabin told me to push the button, "the one on top." The elevator rose with exasperating slowness. It went up four floors, each landing offering the same vista: hallways with worn, stained carpeting, doors open onto vacant rooms. The edges of the wallpaper were peeling, and everywhere were stacks of mattresses and piles of sheets and tablecloths emitting a sharp smell of mildew.

The elevator stopped with an alarming jolt. I stepped out as though released from a cage. There was another hallway covered with wine-colored carpeting just like the others, and at its end the tacit invitation of a door ajar. I went to it but hesitated at the threshold, for the room was sunk in shadow, the only light coming from the gray October sky that seeped through heavy velvet drapes. Once my eyes adjusted to the half-darkness, I tried to survey the room I'd just stepped into.

"Come in, my boy, come in." It was Tabori's voice, unusually cordial. "Did you meet Boris? Try to remember he's a bit hard of hearing." I told him I'd noticed that. "Close the door and sit down," he said. "You can hang your coat in that corner."

I did so, obeying Tabori's voice, though the man had yet to appear. Noises from beyond the back wall suggested a kitchen there, and a moment later Tabori emerged, steaming teapot in hand. "Have you had breakfast, Hans?" It was the first time he'd called me by my first name. "Would you like some tea, biscuits?"

I told him I'd already had breakfast.

"Please excuse me, but I haven't. Make yourself at home," he added as he turned away.

Left alone, I looked around. The size of the room, far larger than the cramped spaces of the rest of the hotel, suggested that the top-floor apartment had once been the imperial suite. But it gave the impression of having been swamped in a sea of debris, so mismatched were the furnishings and knickknacks. They were arranged in layers of disorder, as though a logical, rational system had collapsed, each piece giving way to new arrivals, forced to support other objects that in turn served as platforms for others. Only a hopeless madman—or a chess genius—could live in such chaos. If the ground-floor junk shop belonged to Tabori, he must have kept the best pieces for himself, putting only castoffs up for sale. The room must once have been truly comfortable. The floor was covered with thick antique rugs, and the vintage furniture seemed of excellent construction. In the center of the room, like an island, stood a grand piano on whose lowered lid were dozens of picture frames of all styles and sizes. Hanging on the walls were wooden shelves crammed with books and pamphlets. I paged through one of them. There were bound pages of newspapers, an impressive collection of chess columns, and articles on all aspects of the game, down to the briefest of items referring to it in any way. Finally I stood, entranced, before a wall literally covered with pictures—oils, drawings, watercolors, and tempera that brought to mind artists like Chagall, Munch, and Kandinsky. The works weren't famous, but each one's style was readily recognizable. I naturally assumed them to be brilliantly executed fakes; had they been real, the collection would have been priceless. I was so absorbed in my contemplation of these marvels that I didn't notice Tabori standing behind me.

"Do you like painting?"

"I'm a student at the Academy of Fine Arts," I responded with some pride, though the meager results I'd achieved so far certainly offered no grounds for it. "They're not real, are they?" I asked, intending the comment as a mere quip, certainly not expecting him to reply that they were "all genuine, every last one of them." Noting my astonishment, he winked and added, "Though it's probably better to keep that to yourself."

Without offering me a seat, Tabori sat down on a stool and proceeded to a calm but intense interrogation. He was apparently determined to confirm things he already knew, and I thought he tried to conceal a certain satisfaction when I reported I was an orphan with no relatives but my grandmother.

"You know," he said, "when I was a child I could tell how much influence the game had over the person I was talking to, just by staring at him here, in the middle of the forehead." Then suddenly he clapped his hands as though regretting having shared that information and eager to change the subject. "Okay," he exclaimed, "let's go to work." He looked me up and down as though pondering what sort of outfit I needed for my new role. "By the way," he said, "would you rather be a hero or an antihero?"

When I told him I had no idea what he meant, he tried to explain it to me. "Look," he said, "according to the psychoanalyst Reuben Fine, one of the world's greatest players, players are of two antithetical types. One is the hero, who has no religion, no reason for being, other than chess. His every satisfaction and every pleasure is drawn from the board and the victories it brings him; conversely, his every pain and fear of death is embodied in his defeats. The hero cannot imagine existence outside the battlefield of chess. He cannot exist without struggle, for it alone sustains him, and he loses all interest in his surroundings when his preeminence begins to fade. Since for him nothing else exists, he vanishes, if not physically (since death may come only decades later), at least as an individual. This, of course, is the most risky path . . ."

I was disturbed by Tabori's words, for they described my symptoms perfectly, and he spoke gravely, as if discussing a terrible illness. Was I already infected so badly? But I still had hope.

"And the antihero?"

"The antihero can also be among the greatest of players, even a world champion, like Lasker, for instance, except that he isn't predestined for it. He doesn't sell his soul to the devil unconditionally, but slips in an escape clause or two. He doesn't live for chess *alone,* if you see what I mean. He's a man, too, and as such retains freedom of choice. Lasker was a mathematician and philosopher, an amateur musician, and, they say, an excellent bridge player as well."

This category seemed better suited to me. After all, I loved painting, I liked girls . . . but just the same, losing a game was like death.

Tabori seemed to read my mind. "For your sake, I dearly hope you belong to the second category, but it may be too early to tell. One way or the other, you'll find out on your own." He then uttered a mysterious phrase, almost to himself:

"I hope the time has come for the human race to turn its back on every variety of demigod."

I couldn't ask him to explain this last remark, since he was already signaling me to follow him.

He started for a door at the other end of the room. As we passed the piano I glanced at the collection of picture frames and felt an irrepressible chill at the photographs they contained.

Tabori led me down a hallway entirely covered by a multicolored carpet of Oriental design to a small room about nine feet square, completely bare and lit only by a kind of skylight. In the middle of the room was a platform, and on the platform stood a sinister square table in whose center was a metal chessboard with metal pieces. It almost looked like a gallows for a prisoner sentenced to "play by the neck until dead." The pieces, the black an alloy of bronze, the white of silver, were clearly of excellent construction. They gleamed coldly, having neither the smoothness of plastic nor the warmth of wood. They seemed bare, the distillation of the lethal essence of a sword.

They were arranged in a complex mid-game position that seemed vaguely familiar.

"Recognize it?" Tabori asked.

"I'm not sure; I think . . ." At first I couldn't remember, but as I looked more closely, I suddenly recalled the game I'd been playing the night Tabori stood at my table and I so rashly disappointed him. I was disconcerted that he'd been able to retain such a complicated position after a single glance, and I swelled with pride that he'd considered it interesting enough to memorize.

"I should have moved the pawn," I admitted contritely.

"Well, you were in too much of a hurry. You fell into the

trap of your own vanity. But suppose, just for a moment, that very high stakes had been involved. Would you have taken the risk in that case?"

"I don't think so."

Now that I looked calmly at the board, all nervous tension gone, I saw how easily I could have won. The modest pawn advance would have established an impregnable defense, and though my opponent would have preserved material parity, he would have soon faced zugzwang: any move he made would have turned against him.

"Whatever you say," Tabori continued, "chess is always a game, albeit of a very special kind, and as such there should always be stakes. The greater the stakes, the sharper your attention. For some individuals fear of defeat is motivation enough, but not all have the hero's inordinate pride, not all suffer defeat with equal intensity. Their pain is brief, and too soon forgotten. And of course it can be mitigated by countless excuses—distraction, weariness, overconfidence in facing a weaker opponent. Then there are born losers, who always nurture disaster within themselves."

I would have said that my greatest defect was impatience, but Tabori disagreed.

"Your defect is lack of attention," he thundered, uttering the last phrase like a jail sentence. "And you're not alone. It's every player's greatest defect. And when I say attention, I mean something far greater than is commonly thought. In their holy festivals the Mayan priests competed in a game similar to modern jai alai, but as they grasped and hurled the ball, they believed that the slightest error would cause the sun to fall from the sky. That's the kind of attention I'm talking about, as though your own life were at stake—or, rather, not just your own, since you might be a potential suicide, but also the life of every person dear to you. All else is secondary. Strategy, tactics, the study of openings and endgames—useless in the absence of this kind of attention. I refer, of course, to high-level play, at the master's level, not to the squalid exhibitions to which I'm so often treated at our club."

Tabori had been talking for quite a while now, but it was as though I were seeing him for the first time, as though the words he'd just spoken had altered his features.

He was wearing a silk robe trimmed with gold, and slippers with the toes slightly turned up. It gave him a Levantine look. His cheeks were dark, as though powdered with coal dust, making a stark contrast to the pallor of his brow. Though he was freshly shaved, the shadow of his beard could be seen high on his cheekbones. Had he let it grow, it would have covered his face with rich curls, like Gilgamesh's. That feature removed any hope that I might one day resemble him, blondish adolescent as I was, with no more than a peach fuzz.

He'd begun to set up the pieces as he talked, and this inclined me to assume that he was about to give me my first lesson. And so he was, though not exactly as I expected. After placing the final piece on the board, he removed his own queen and said, "You play white. Make your move."

He was giving me an incredible advantage. Playing without your queen is like going into a boxing match with a hand tied behind your back. And as if that wasn't humiliating enough, I watched with astonishment as he turned the back of his chair to the table and announced he would forgo looking at the board. I would tell him my move, he would tell me his, and I would move both his pieces and mine. At first I found the proposal mortifying, but now, paradoxically, it seems amusing. He'd be playing not only with one hand tied behind his back but also blindfold. The challenge he set for himself seemed almost like a magic trick.

The game began. I expected to be able to strike when and where I pleased. For an instant it even occurred to me that I could cheat. We were playing without time limits. Tabori sat with his back to me, lighting a cigarette every now and then, staring at a blank wall, upon which he seemed to see more than I did on the board. The game lasted late into the afternoon, at which point Tabori announced that he had initiated a forced sequence that would lead to victory in seven moves. Since he still had his back to me, the irony of fate had it that it was my task to demonstrate his claim by moving the pieces until I was checkmated.

Such was my master's harsh first lesson, and it crushed my self-esteem. If I could be beaten in this manner, how many thousands of light-years was I from the ideal I meant to attain?

I left the building as though roused from a nightmare that tormented me even after waking. I remember nothing of our leave-taking or of my journey back to my student lodgings. I was envious of my roommate who didn't know a knight from a bishop, and I picked up my art history books again, finding bitter comfort in the thought that there was more to life than chess.

My wounded pride ached for many days. At the idea of chess I felt only boundless nausea. Naturally, I stayed away from the Rote Engel.

Had I followed those momentary impulses, mine would

have been the shortest career in the history of the game. But you know as well as I do that it is not we who decide how and when to abandon chess but chess that rules us. Nevertheless, I did stay away from the club for some time, not even wishing to lay eyes on a board. Then one day I sat down and tried to reconstruct the game in which I'd suffered such humiliating defeat, and I concluded that if it had really gone the way I now remembered, I'd been a complete fool. This was not the way I played. One thing was certain: I had to rethink everything with greater rigor. I set myself a deadline and began to go through the many books I'd inherited from my father, books that, until then, I'd been presumptuous enough to consider superfluous. I began to study the games of the great masters, seeking to appropriate their secrets. When I returned to the club after several weeks of arduous study, the wound had healed to the point that I was ready to compete with anyone, even Tabori—and this time I would spot *him* a queen!

But there was no sign of him. No one had seen him for more than a week. Someone said he'd gone to Switzerland for an important tournament, someone else that he had health problems. I returned to the Fischer Pension, where I was admitted by Boris, the man who was hard of hearing. He didn't seem at all happy to see me. He told me no one knew when Tabori might return. I was about to give up when he handed me an envelope Tabori had left for me. On it he'd written: "That you might think better." Inside was a clipping from a local newspaper, the headline underscored in red. It was a story about an accident. A bus carrying schoolchildren on a class trip had fallen from a bridge. Two were dead, dozens seriously hurt. I read and reread the article, finding no connection either to myself or to Tabori, or, for that matter, to chess. I wasn't sure what to think, and had just about decided it was a mistake of some kind when I happened to turn over the page and noticed something written in a tiny but clear handwriting, a phrase that cost me several nights' sleep: "What if this had been caused by your inattention?"

I don't remember how long that sentence—or perhaps I should call it an accusation—echoed in my brain. I understood it was meant to be purely symbolic, but it had the force of a slander, depriving me of any chance to protest my innocence precisely because of its metaphysical character. Indeed, how can we ever be sure that our behavior, or even merely our thought, has not unwittingly engendered catastrophe?

I was dying to ask Tabori himself for an explanation, but his absence persisted. The tournament in Switzerland had ended some time ago, and there was still no sign of him.

Then suddenly he reappeared at the club one evening, greeted by applause, the members gathering around him. With the aid of a wall board he demonstrated and commented on several of the most beautiful games he'd seen at the tournament, games free of mistakes and blunders, victories won by razor-thin differences. Tabori gave me the book issued by the tournament organizers with the record of all the games played. He invited me to join him the following Sunday, if I still wanted to.

All this time I'd been eagerly awaiting his return so that I could ask him to explain his sibylline message, but when I found myself back in his apartment, I decided not to mention it, sensing that this was what he expected. Besides, the truth is that as I pondered the sentence he'd written, I sensed an inner awakening to the Attention he'd spoken of so gravely. It had even gone beyond chess, to the world around me. It was a question of *seeing* instead of merely *looking,* a goal pursued by many philosophers. I sensed that this was part of his teaching and that he expected me to accept it without reservation.

It was another rainy Sunday, and the ritual was unchanged, including the long wait out on the street. I was shown into the same room. I took off my overcoat. Tabori puttered around in the kitchen.

As I waited I went to the piano to take a closer look at the faces displayed in those precious frames. The first time I'd refrained from doing so, almost as if fearing to violate a tacit taboo. Why did I feel such emptiness when I glanced at them? I went closer, barely controlling a tremor that shook my whole body. I stood immobile in their presence.

The photographs were arranged in groups as if of an extended family, though they seemed completely alien to one another, with nothing in common except the luminous blindness that only portraits of the dead seem to acquire. I could see no tie of kinship between the female schoolteacher with the pallid, oval face and the mustachioed peasant, nor between the corpulent working-class woman and the mild philosopher with the thick eyeglasses. Yet something bound them together. How many were there? More than two dozen, it seemed. A strange mixture of features, races, shapes, and cultures, sharing only a general feeling of tragedy. The paper itself seemed to have suffered, curled as though wounded, stained by blood or mud.

I wondered what they meant to him. Surely something important, judging by the care with which he had arranged the miniature graveyard of memory in which my gaze continued to wander as though seeking an enigma I was meant to resolve. But some things are best grasped without the sense of sight. As I penetrated deeper into that forest of faces in search of a path leading somewhere, I was struck again and far more strongly by the painful feeling of having to abandon not merely a fragment but a wide zone of my being, one that spread steadily, dark and changeable as quicksand. At that moment—I don't know what I saw or what I guessed—the blood rushed to my head with a rumble like kettledrums, and against the background of what I thought I was looking at passed a rapid sequence of unbelievable atrocities, frightful, revolting scenes in an endless chain. I was deafened by the roar of my own blood. It was as though a chorus had risen from those faces, suddenly suffused with a powerful aspiration to exist.

I forced myself to take a step backward just as Tabori came into the room. I didn't want him to see that I'd been staring, but my anxiety did not pass unnoticed. "What you're looking at is an altar," he said gravely, "an altar to absence, to the death of the spirit."

He motioned me to follow him, and as we passed the piano he paused for a moment to glance at the photographs as if checking that none was out of place.

We returned to the cell. The board was in the position in which we'd left it last time. It almost made me nauseous to look at it. Tabori asked me to set up the pieces.

I forgot to mention that these metal figures were quite heavy and bulky. Their bases were not smooth but had projections like the clips of a cartridge. The board had holes that matched the projections, making it impossible to place a piece anywhere but in the exact center of a square.

To my great surprise, Tabori wanted to play an even game, without conceding me so much as a pawn. I was proud of this unexpected gesture of respect, and began to play with great accuracy. I had white, and the defense Tabori played, a variation of the Indian defense, had been known in theory and practice for more than half a century—until he stepped off the beaten path and sacrificed a knight to unleash a counterattack on the queen's side. Complications soon proliferated, and the atmosphere in the tiny cell was laden with tension. For quite a while I was able to retain the initiative, even winning another pawn. I saw a way to launch a forced sequence that would result in further material gains, perhaps even victory.

The game now reached a critical phase. This time I had no reason to believe that Tabori wanted to go easy on me. But I had a clear advantage, and I sensed that the decisive move was near. All my energy was focused on the effort to identify a winning sequence, but it continued to elude me, like a person who looms up out of a fog, letting himself be glimpsed momentarily only to vanish. I gathered from the expression on his face that Tabori was tacitly warning me: the game was in my grasp; I must not let it slip away.

The time I took to ponder what move to make seemed wrenched from reality. It could not be measured in minutes, by the chiming of hours or the ticking of a clock or the winding down of any mechanism, for it was pure present, as in a spaceship hurtling along at the speed of light, time standing still for me while centuries flew by on the planet I'd left behind.

Every choice automatically implies the abandonment of alternatives. We'd be immortal if we weren't forced to make choices, and in the end I, too, had to submit to this rule.

Even now I can still see the succession of instants that elapsed between the making of my choice and its execution, like a sequence of slides depicting motion to a predetermined end, as sometimes happens in dreams where cause and effect are reversed to incorporate a real event that awakens us.

Suddenly my hand materializes. Driven by a constellation of neurons presumably centered somewhere in my brain's right hemisphere, it moves toward a certain piece—I can see the horse's head even now, thrown back as if the animal were caught in the act of rearing. I snatch the piece from its column and replace it in an adjoining one.

My entire life, all its events great and small, all its joys and afflictions, seems to float atop a stagnant, murky surface in which things are not always where they seem to be when you look at them, in which nothing is clear or consistent or logical or even simply linked to other things, in which nothing has delineated boundaries or fully perceptible forms—nothing except that position on the board, which even now burns in my memory with a light of its own, as I imagine the burning bush remained in the memory of Moses.

I picked up the knight. Nothing happened as I held it in midair, for my choice was not yet made. I might still put the piece down elsewhere (there were at least two other possibilities). But when finally I placed it in the fatal square, I was electrified—and I mean that literally. A terrible shock sprang from the silvery head of that horse, shooting through my arm to the rest of my body and driving me to my feet with a shout. My chair spilled to the floor.

■   ■   ■

The train began to slow down. Baum, who had fallen asleep, suddenly roused himself in his corner.

"Where are we?" he asked in alarm, relaxing when he saw they were pulling into Salzburg.

After a brief stop the train picked up speed again, a comet in the night.

Baum yawned, looked at his watch, and stood up. He put the chess set back in its case and the case back in the valise. He checked that his raincoat was still in its place and settled back to his old position, determined not to sleep again.

Frisch hadn't moved. He'd gone through the formalities at the border with his legs crossed and his arms folded, and now that the train was back up to speed, he seemed ready to hear the rest of Mayer's story, perhaps guessing it had something to do with him.

But Mayer did not begin again immediately. He could not have said how long they sat in silence, perhaps for the interminable time required to ponder a difficult move. It was Frisch who finally asked him to go on, leaning forward from the waist in a barely perceptible gesture that denoted curiosity and perhaps slight apprehension.

"Please continue," he said.

It was the move Mayer had been waiting for. He now felt perfectly at ease, just as he did when he played chess—initial unbearable tension being supplanted by a state of supreme serenity in which everything became clear and coherent and he could lay hold of the future's tiniest nuance.

He thrust his hand into the pocket of his raincoat and fingered the cloth packet like a purse snatcher who, having skillfully executed his theft, furtively assesses his loot with the sense of touch alone. Squeezing it between his fingers, he sensed a kind of muffled rattle. Something was wrapped in the coarse cloth. It might have been coins, except it didn't weigh enough. Hans knew very well what the package contained, and it was just that thought which now convinced him to continue his tale without delay.

I don't know how long I stood there, paralyzed by surprise, fear, and confusion, or perhaps simply clinging to myself. Tabori had ceased to exist. He was a remote, hypothetical entity. I didn't think he could have been the cause of what had just happened. He sat there impassive, an involuntary witness to the attack I'd suffered, an attack he neither shared nor understood—or so I believed.

Somewhere I once read about the training of certain Zen monks, who remain in the most absolute immobility for very long periods, immersed in deep meditation and scrupulously supervised by their masters. Only at the moment most propitious for enlightenment may the master, at his own discretion, deliver a sudden blow with a bamboo cane, an accurate downward stroke right between the eyes of the neophyte now considered mature, just when he least expects it. The result is not always salutary, it seems, but when it is, awakening is accompanied by a sonorous laugh that bursts from the disciple's chest.

Well, something like that happened to me. All at once I was gripped by irrepressible laughter, which, however, failed to infect my master. But there was a particular reason for my laughter. In a flash I traced the effect to the cause, which lay nowhere else but on that chessboard. And the board belonged to Tabori. I wondered whether I hadn't fallen victim to a madman. Only my master's imperturbable air prevented me from taking flight. Although I guessed that I'd just received a warning of some kind, my rational side demanded an explanation.

There was no need to request it. Tabori came over to me, bending to right the chair I'd knocked over and urging me to sit down. The position on the board was intact, and I suddenly realized that my last move had been a monumental blunder.

Tabori, however, said nothing about the game itself, knowing as he did that something else was on my mind.

"It was only a weak move," he said, almost as if trying to reassure me. "But your own tension was too great."

He paused. The glow from the skylight seemed to envelop his face, momentarily transfiguring it. I'd never seen him look like that. It was as though he were no longer there beside me, but had gone elsewhere, very far from that cell.

When he spoke again, his voice was different. He told me this chessboard once belonged to his father. It was lost during the war, and he recovered it only twenty years later, coming upon it by chance among a consignment of otherwise worthless objects purchased by lot when the contents of an old Viennese home were sold off.

It had been handed down in his family for centuries. Legend had it that it was one of the objects infused with a kind of life by Kabbalists—possibly by Abulafia himself. Whether or not there was any truth to that, it definitely produced rapid results, for it punished mistakes instantaneously. Whoever played with it felt pain proportionate to the error committed, eventually coming to feel physical revulsion for any reckless move. Moreover, its effects were persistent, subsequently felt even on ordinary boards. The mind was thus illuminated, and no move would be attempted unless the player was absolutely sure of having assessed its most far-reaching consequences.

"Some time ago you made a request of me, and I replied that much depended on you, on your will to learn. Naturally, you're disconcerted by what just happened, but you said you were ready to do 'anything,' and I accepted your request. You didn't know it, but I'd been keeping an eye on you for some time. I watched how you played, and I was sure you had real talent."

Ah, gentlemen, how relative is the value we ascribe to things, so insignificant compared to our pride! That last phrase erased my every doubt and fear. I believe I even blushed, for I never dreamed I deserved such praise. "But I lost a game where I had a queen advantage," I protested in confusion. "And you couldn't even see the board."

Tabori waved a hand dismissively.

"Meaningless," he said. "I see the board in my mind as clearly as you see it with your eyes. And as for the handicap, the truth is I was the one who had the advantage in that game, however paradoxical that might seem."

"I don't understand."

"Look, the game of chess—or rather, the arrangement of the pieces in the game—is like the disposition of furniture in an apartment you've lived in for years: an armchair here, a stool there, a table in the middle of the room. If the placement of these objects is altered, if one piece of furniture is taken from the place it has long occupied, you feel ill at ease. Accustomed to moving in a well-known space, you continue to act as though everything were still where it belongs, and sooner or later you stumble over a console or fall on your rear end trying to sit on a chair that's been moved.

"The disadvantage you faced was to have to play with your pieces arranged as though my queen were still present. You made the usual moves, not realizing that since this piece had been removed, it was possible to attack in a different way. And since you thought I couldn't see the board, you tried to lure me into childish traps, unaware that the board was before my eyes no less than yours. I'm sure it would be different if we played another game like that."

Given my status as disciple, I thought it best to keep silent.

"Do you know how many years it's been since I gave up chess?" he asked after a very long pause.

"No . . ."

He then told me that our game had been his first in more than forty years. I found that hard to believe, though neither I nor anyone else had ever seen him contend against an opponent of his own.

Nothing brings us closer to another person than the sharing of a secret, and my pride, already amply gratified, now received a final, unexpected gift.

"I would like to start playing again," he said, "but you will do so in my place."

He stood and left the room. When he returned several minutes later, he was wearing his overcoat.

"Come," he said. "There's something else we have to do. Something I have to show you. It won't take long. We'll be back in two hours."

Boris was waiting for us at the wheel of an ancient Mercedes, the engine running. We sat in the back, and the car set out in the rain. I couldn't imagine where we were going, and didn't dare ask. After a long silence Tabori asked me whether I'd ever seen a dead body.

The question chilled me. I told him no, I didn't think I ever had.

"You've never been to a funeral?"

I said I'd once walked in a funeral procession, as a child.

"Your parents' funeral?"

No, I said, that of a distant relative. They'd kept me away from my parents' funeral. I was too young, and they tried to hide the tragedy from me. Perhaps a year after they died, my grandmother finally told me, with the requisite caution, that my parents had been killed in an accident.

Boris exited the Ring and joined the traffic on Lazarettgasse, the street that leads to Vienna's general hospital. I thought we were going to visit someone. Perhaps a friend or relative of Tabori's was seriously ill.

But we didn't stop at the hospital. Instead we skirted part of its outer wall and went around it, finally turning into a dead-end street and stopping in front of a squat brick building with iron gratings on the windows and a large outer gate. Waiting for us was an amazingly thin old man in a gray lab coat that hung from his shoulders as from a hanger. Boris stayed in the car. Tabori and I went through a portal cut into the massive outer gate. There was a covered entranceway, and then we ran through the rain across a narrow courtyard to another entranceway just like the first. We went down a long stairway into a hallway, and then another, and yet another, all of them faintly lit by feeble fluorescent bulbs so widely spaced that at some points we were almost in darkness. The man guided us through an underground labyrinth of corridors. A sharp smell of formaldehyde told me what kind of place this was. I looked at Tabori, who replied with a reassuring glance. At the end of the last and longest corridor was a door.

The man took a key from his pocket, opened the door, and led us into a large room tiled all the way to its high ceiling. The grates at the top edges of the walls confirmed my stifling impression that we were well below ground level. Every noise (the closing of the iron door, our footsteps on the floor) was wildly amplified by the tall bare walls, violating the absolute silence these sepulchral surroundings seemed to demand. The man escorted us to the far end of the room, to a chrome-plated gurney on which the inert outline of a body was visible under a gray sheet. Alongside was a trolley-cart with several shelves bearing dissecting tools. The man looked at Tabori, at me, and finally at the gray sheet, spotted on one side by a cluster of dark stains. He stared at it as though able to see through it. "Twenty years old," he said. "Found dead last night. Probable cause: fracture of the skull consequent to a fall, presumably from the fifth floor of an apartment building." He gripped the edge of the sheet and uncovered the body.

I felt like a different person as we drove back through a downpour that sorely tested the windshield wipers. I would have had trouble remembering my name had anyone asked it. Tabori delivered a long monologue on why this excursion had been necessary. He said he wanted to be sure I'd understand his story when the time came to tell me why he hadn't played chess in more than forty years.

"If ever I speak to you of the dead," he concluded, "I want to be sure you know what I'm talking about."

The stifling memory of the place we'd just left suddenly assailed me. The smell of our wet clothes aroused an irrepressible attack of nausea. I asked them to let me out. Boris pulled over on the Mariahilfer Strasse, and the car drove off, leaving me dazed at the curbside. I felt as though I'd just returned from a long journey or emerged from total amnesia, as though I'd been wrenched out of time and dropped back in somewhere else. It reminded me of the legend of the monk who dozed off during prayers and woke up a century later.

It was dark when I reached the subway station. The rain had stopped, and the streets were suddenly crowded. Traffic flowed like a long, rainbow-colored caterpillar. Nothing seemed to have changed except me.

My training began that day and continued for more than a year. The tiny cell on the top floor of the Fischer Pension became my refuge and prison. Little remained of the outside world, which gradually seemed to dissolve. A body that resembled mine attended classes, paid occasional visits to my grandmother, ate, slept, and walked around as usual, but I was always within that cell, struggling with myself. I assure you, it wasn't easy. That chessboard, which Tabori euphemistically called propaedeutic, was a true instrument of torture. Playing on it was like walking through a minefield. Not that the voltage was high; the shocks I felt when I made mistakes were barely stronger than those you would get from static electricity, but their threat was hard to take, especially in the early days, when my errors were more frequent. Tabori never bothered to correct me, never told me whether I'd made a good move or a bad one, never taught me strategy or tactics or an opening or an endgame. For the first few months he never even spoke to me at all. He simply had me play. He would sit motionless across the board from me, embodying in his impassivity the worst sort of player you could face. He moved his pieces with exasperating slowness, almost as if trying to stamp the full destructive potential of every move on my mind. It's amazing how different the same move can be when made by two different players, even the very first move, so well known to everyone, including those who have just learned the rules. The motion is the same, the pawn moves forward onto the same square. But where for the beginner it's only a move, for the master it becomes the first step in a long sequence. It's like the difference between two apparently identical musical notes that might begin a nursery rhyme or a symphony. Nor could I ever tell from his expression if or when a shock would come. Not even the vaguest of suggestions could be gleaned from his gestures. I had to concentrate on the game alone, transcending matter and penetrating appearances so as to enter a world of pure mental energy. When I attained this dimension—and I crossed the threshold more and more often—that universe imbued with its own energy would have continued to pulse on its own even if I closed my eyes and let the board be taken away.

As I say, it wasn't easy. I often left that room and that building on the verge of nervous collapse. The electric-shock punishments, now increasingly rare, were a kind of reminder that I was still alive, still human. Paradoxically, they actually eased the state of constant tension.

More than once I came close to giving up, but finally I became so dependent that the idea of abandoning the training was inconceivable. I even thirsted for more, wishing I could return more and more often to that ideal world in which counterposed polarities constantly strove to merge with and annihilate each other. At first this state of consciousness lasted for fleeting instants, after which I would sink back into darkness, but as my training continued, the flashes of enlightenment became increasingly frequent and long-lasting, finally forming a continuum in which I could immerse myself and remain as long as I chose, without the slightest fatigue, indeed in a state of divine, ineffable calm. Once I attained that state, there was not the remotest chance I'd make a mistake. I became imbued with a sense of omnipotence and invincibility. Anything that fell short of perfection was error. Moves merely neutral or passive, neither completely bad nor completely good, were punished equally. All proportions guarded, I had the sense that the merest oversight (in the unlikely event I might still commit one) would surely cost me my life.

But there was something else as well. I came to see the game as a living thing, a magically produced organism that, once it came to life, developed a kind of instinct for self-preservation. It was a complex of colors such as would appear in a spectrogram, and I had to take it in hand like a surgeon, cutting and sewing muscles and arteries, paying the most careful attention to what I was doing. Its claim to its own right to exist was asserted with ever greater force, and exactly for that reason I was increasingly afraid of destroying it with a misplaced move. Though infinitely less complex than a human organism, so often and so easily tortured and killed by its fellows, it, too, felt genuine pain, and if I was unfortunate enough to damage a vital organ, there was a sudden loss of energy and an immediate consequent pain, passed on to me in the form of an electrical discharge. I continued to feel this even afterward, when Tabori assured me that no current had flowed and what I felt was merely a mental impulse.

Entering the field of battle seemed easy after all this, and I soon accumulated enough points to be admitted to the biggest tournaments, though I still hadn't earned my official master's ranking. I played against masters and grand masters of all countries. Tabori and I spent more than a year traveling throughout Europe, never missing a single tournament. If two happened to be held at the same time, he would pick the one he considered more important.

He acted as my aide, analyzing suspended games, preparing variations for me to play, sometimes suggesting openings and defenses to use against particular opponents. He knew their habits and styles, their strong and weak points. His memory was so formidable he could recall all the games of the greatest players. For him it was like recognizing a face with features so distinct it was difficult to forget even if he'd seen it only once. Often he was able to reproduce the most minute details of a variation that had been played decades earlier.

As for myself, I now enjoyed an infallible instinct. If I was about to make not a mistaken but simply a weak move, I could have sworn the piece I was preparing to touch glowed with a bluish light, like St. Elmo's fire on the flagstaffs of a ship when a storm approaches. Tabori's presence was of course an immense help to me, even though the rules did not allow us to confer during a game. It was enough to know he was there. Courage filled me at the mere sight of him, as though his power and knowledge could be transmitted to me even from a distance.

There was just one inflexible condition to our companionship: Tabori insisted that whenever white opened with the queen's gambit, I had to play a certain variation he'd taught me down to the smallest detail. It involved a knight sacrifice that plunged the game into chaos, but if you were aware of the consequences, you could emerge victorious eight times out of ten. I won prizes for the best game in tournaments by playing this variation. Tabori was especially attached to it, often telling me that it was his contribution to the history of chess.

Our European forays lasted for more than a year. It was a time of superhuman tension that nevertheless afforded me moments of genuine happiness.

Until one day Tabori disappeared. There'd been no hint it would end like this, except that in those last days he seemed tired and tense, apparently on the edge of sharing some secret with me but never quite able to summon the courage to do so.

He left me an envelope containing a sum of money and a note urging me not to lose faith in him. He said he had to go away because his health no longer allowed him to lead such a turbulent life. He also said that if there was any possibility of attaining the goal he'd set, either it had already been reached or any further effort would be futile. What he meant by this was a mystery to me.

We were in Baden-Baden at the close of the tourist season. The tournament was the parting gesture of a year now ending with the first autumn rains. I don't think even his death would have cast me into the despair caused by his inexplicable disappearance. The pain of his absence was sharpened by the feeling of betrayal. That was the hardest thing to surmount. I locked myself in my room for two whole days and might never have come out if the obviously worried hotel manager hadn't used his passkey to burst into my room with a police officer. It was all quite embarrassing, but he apologized once he saw that nothing was amiss, treating me with all due respect. The mere fact that I was a chess player seemed to clarify many things for him. He told me the hotel was closing up for the winter. That same afternoon I boarded a train back to Vienna.

I returned to a tragedy: my grandmother had killed herself after being jilted by a young man only a few years my senior, choosing to die in the theatrical manner in which she'd lived. On her way home from a party one night she had the taxi stop, descended the steps of one of the many bridges over the Danube, and—or so I imagine—cast herself into the river's waters.

The body was recovered twenty days later, entangled in a lock. She was still wearing her evening gown. The poor woman had tried to end her life gloriously, but careful as she was about her appearance, she hadn't realized that her body would be devoured by the river and her suicide's corpse further ravaged by the medical examiner's scalpel.

The house, along with its contents and furnishings, was seized and auctioned to satisfy her many creditors. Little of her remained to me: just a few letters documenting her tragic passion.

I don't know what I would have done without the money Tabori left me. I spent some of it to place a headstone in the potter's field where my grandmother was buried. The rest didn't last long. In the end I was reduced to making sketches of customers in beer halls for spare change. The few schillings I asked for were usually supplemented by the offer of a stein, which of course I couldn't refuse. Often I returned to my room in the middle of the night dead drunk, tired, and hungry.

It was as though I'd flirted with success only to end my life at the age of twenty. All I felt was anger at everyone who'd abandoned me: my parents, my grandmother, and most of all Tabori.

I returned to my old haunts solely to subject myself to unbearable nostalgia. The city seemed to have changed in the past year, and I sometimes wondered whether it had really been only a year or whether time was now measured in other units. The Fischer Pension was completely deserted. A sign on the façade announced the building's imminent demolition. The Rote Engel, which I entered only once, had also changed completely. The management, club members, and even my old opponent Strumpfel Lump were gone as though dead, or as though they had never existed. Sometimes I doubted whether I had ever met Tabori and his miraculous chessboard (indeed, who would have believed it?). I even doubted myself: had I truly been so passionately carried away by a game the mere thought of which now filled me with dread?

One night I returned to my room to find the door padlocked and my meager belongings piled on the landing. I was four months behind in the rent, and the landlord had taken decisive action. From that night on, my lodgings were the street, or sometimes a public shelter for the city's outcasts that opened at ten at night and closed at seven in the morning. During the day I wandered aimlessly in a resplendent and hostile Vienna, lacking all hope.

I hadn't touched a chess set since my master's disappearance, and I feared I would never play again. This dread was confirmed one day when I happened into a low-life tavern near the riverbank, hungry and hoping to find a customer willing to pose for one of my caricatures. But the place was empty. When I called out, no one answered. Just then I noticed a little table a few steps away, with a chess set abandoned by someone who had left the pieces scattered. I forced myself to sit down at the table, just to see if I was still capable of playing. But it was an effort merely to pick up the pieces and place them on the right squares. A lethal weariness swept over me. The room went dark, and everything around me began to undulate as though it were painted on a curtain being shaken by an unexpected gust of wind. At that moment drops of blood rained onto the board, falling one beside the other in rapid succession like silent explosions. Gripped by panic, I leaped to my feet and fled from the tavern, holding my hands to my bleeding face and overturning the table and the board. Since then I've never had the heart to play again.

Here Mayer fell silent, waiting to see how his audience of two would react to his tale.

"Did you ever see Tabori again?"

It was Baum who spoke. He had put on his raincoat as the train approached the station and was now sitting on the edge of his seat, his briefcase clasped between his knees. His question was a pure act of courtesy containing no sign of genuine interest, and Hans didn't answer it. Baum gazed impatiently out the window at the now familiar landscape. When the train began to slow down, he stood and opened the sliding door to the corridor, where passengers had begun lining up.

"Really a very interesting story," he said, again with vacuous politeness. "A pity I must leave you now." He turned to Frisch. "See you next Tuesday," he said. "You can tell me the rest then."

Frisch raised a hand in farewell but did not reply. Baum shook as the train crossed over a switch. When it entered the station, he stepped decisively into the corridor. They watched him get off and walk hurriedly past their window toward the exit.

No one else came into the compartment when the train began to move again. Hans pulled the door shut and sat in the seat Baum had vacated, thus placing himself across from Frisch like an opponent preparing to move to a rapid endgame.

Frisch noted the maneuver. Nearly starting in surprise, he glanced at his watch to conceal his annoyance. "Exactly on time," he said. "At midnight we'll be in Vienna."

They were silent for several minutes, but something seemed to hang in that silence.

Vienna, Mayer thought, squeezing the object concealed in his pocket. At that moment it assumed its full meaning, proof of an act of evil in a distant past. The temptation to take it out was nearly irresistible, as in earlier days he'd sometimes been unable to resist a premature move that would ruin his whole game. But he'd learned his lesson. He summoned his strength. He must not act sooner than planned. He had to be patient until they got to Vienna.

His antagonist interrupted his thoughts. For some time Frisch seemed to be wondering whose move it was, and he now uttered Mayer's name under his breath several times, as if trying to remember something. "Mayer . . . Mayer . . . Hans Mayer

. . . I seem to recall a Mayer about whom there was some talk in Hamburg last year, and about two months later in Hastings, if I'm not mistaken, and also during an open in Venice . . ."

"You have an excellent memory."

"I wrote quite a lot about those games. And certainly not fondly. So it was you. And then that sudden withdrawal. I gather you consider yourself a failure who won't ever be able to play again?"

"No, I don't think I ever will."

"You have a weak character."

"Perhaps so."

Frisch gestured vaguely, waving his hand in the air as though renouncing any attempt to express the inexpressible. "For chess you need nerves of steel. And after training with that madman, well . . . It's true, chess can sometimes make you feel omnipotent, as I know very well. I, too, played passionately for many years, and even now, old as I am, the game absorbs almost all my time, or at least almost all my thoughts. When I'm with friends, or even at a meeting at work, I sometimes realize I'm not absorbing what's being said around me, as though a membrane were separating me from the others. At that point chess is no longer an abstract presence but a concrete entity, exactly like a diaphragm dividing me from the world, and like a diaphragm it moves and throbs . . ."

Frisch suddenly stared at Mayer with the expression only old people assume when they are about to speak of their past.

"But you know," he said, his forehead breaking out in reddish blotches, "I might have been world champion."

When Mayer said nothing, Frisch amended his assertion with an abrupt snort. "Granted, they weren't the best of times to devote oneself to such an endeavor, but there were many promising players in Germany who might have taken Alekhine's place, and if it hadn't been for a war that robbed us of our youth . . . well, why not? I truly believe I could have contended for the world title." Frisch fell silent, his brow suddenly furrowed, as if weighing the truth of what he'd just said. "Like the arts, chess seems to hold out the possibility of surviving physical death, of gaining eternal fame. What wouldn't we give to see our name recorded in the annals of the game! All you need is a single game, one variation, one flash of originality. You, for instance, were in some sense the deliberate victim of a careerist who ruined your talent simply to peddle that contemptible variation."

"Well, that's not exactly how it was."

"Tabori. Never even heard of him. The name is probably as fake as the man. The world of chess is unfortunately peopled by the oddest individuals. It's always been that way, though there was a time when the game enjoyed greater, let's say, formal respect. Or at least a time when certain dress codes were observed, unlike today, when tournaments can look like gatherings of hoodlums. Still, a man as bizarre as this Tabori . . . Never heard of anything like that before. Parts of your story seem hard to believe, you know. That electric board, for example. Sounds like science fiction. The Soviets surely would have loved it, what with their methods and their mania for supremacy. A board like that would be the jewel of my collection, if it really existed. Can you imagine? The 'board of pain.' I'd pay any price for it."

"Any price?"

"Any price."

Mayer assessed the request. "I can get it for you," he said.

Frisch gave a start and repeated, "Any price."

"I'm not interested in money."

"Anything else."

"Well," Mayer said, "the 'board of pain,' as you call it, could be in your hands as soon as tomorrow. In fact, consider it yours. All I ask in return is that you listen to the rest of my story."

Frisch chuckled.

"My dear sir," he said, "I am far too old to be taken for a ride. That board is a figment of your imagination." But he was reluctant to abandon belief completely. "If you'd ever seen anything of the kind, it must have been . . . well, let's call it the fruit of a well-contrived suggestion."

"Suppose it was," Mayer replied. "Suggestions can heal . . . or kill. Let's not underestimate them. In any case, the reaction to the mistake always springs from one's own being. Besides which, it's not the means that count but the ends."

"Meaning that you lied to me?"

"The individual conscience is an inconfutable reality—that much is true."

Frisch was already annoyed at having been drawn so ingenuously into this game He had no intention of becoming involved in a philosophical discussion, and he cut Mayer off.

"Of course, of course. Perhaps you were so suggestible as to believe anything. But tell me, did you ever see this Tabori character again?"

I can say with assurance that in Hans Mayer's gaze there now gleamed the deep satisfaction of a player who sees his plan materializing on the board move by move and thinks to himself, This is it! From here on, it was a matter of pure technique, with no need for improvisation or genius.

Like a musician, Mayer paused for a fermata before replying, then began again. "I had news of Tabori just recently. I was in a beer hall peddling my sketches with the usual lack of success when someone grabbed me by the shoulder. It was none other than Boris, last survivor of the Fischer Pension. I have to admit, it was the first time I was glad to see him.

" 'Where have you been hiding?' he asked in a tone of reproach and relief. 'I've been looking for you for months. Tabori is not well. That's why he left you. But he sent me to find you. Good Lord,' he exclaimed, examining me from head to foot, 'how have you come to this?'

"I raised my eyes and saw my reflection in a large mirror. I couldn't argue with him. I looked bad, and judging by the way his nose twitched, I must not have smelled very good either.

"Boris was very decisive. He gave me some money. He told me to 'get rid of those rags' right away. Tabori needed to see me urgently. To make sure I wasted no time, he waited for me at a public bath, then sat in an armchair at the first barbershop we passed, reading the paper while I had a shave and a haircut. Finally he took me to a clothing store where he selected and bought a few items for me. We had a quick bite to eat and then set out.

"Our destination was a rest home on the Bodensee where Tabori was recuperating after what Boris called a nasty operation. He'd lost so much weight I almost didn't recognize him. His hair and beard, which I remembered as dark, had turned gray. He had a room of his own overlooking the lake. He had plenty of books and magazines, as well as a tape recorder and writing materials. Were it not for the canister of oxygen at his bedside, it might have been an ordinary hotel room.

"I was unable to contain my emotion. He held me in an embrace bonier than I remembered. 'Sit down, son,' he said. I drew a chair up to the bed. When Boris left us alone, Tabori began to talk. He said he'd left me without a word only because his health had suddenly deteriorated. He asked me to forgive him. He had little time left to live, and he'd asked a lawyer to initiate adoption proceedings. He'd decided to adopt me before he died and to leave all his paintings to me."

"The story seems to have a happy ending, then," Frisch commented.

"Unfortunately not."

"Why, what happened?"

"Tabori told me that the rest of his property would be willed to an otherwise unidentified 'organization devoted to the search for missing persons.' He then told me for the first time of a man he'd been seeking for decades. Chess was the only thread that might lead to him, and Tabori had used chess to track him down. It was thanks to me that he'd found him. He asked me to forgive him for this, too. He'd used me as a pawn, and he warned me to be careful. Things were still in play, he said, and I would have to finish the game. There was much I had to know, and he would now tell me his story, as he'd once promised. It was a story I would have to repeat to this man. That was the only way he'd be able to remember Tabori."

"And I suppose I am that man," Frisch said.

But let us leave that train to its journey. The pine forest presses close, turning the windows into mirrors, making it seem as though two reflected figures are riding a ghost train on a parallel track, sitting across from each other on high plush seats, frozen as if locked in a chess game while hurtling unscathed through the ruinous shadows of the night. They are less than an hour from Vienna now—just enough time for Hans to bring his endgame to a close by telling *my* story to the man concealed behind the name of Frisch.

Among the qualities a good chess player needs are patience and tenacity. These, indeed, I have never lacked. But decades fly by when we pursue an aim unrelentingly. Fear of failure mounts by the moment. Here the bloodline had been severed, so completion of the task fell to Hans, my son adopted in extremis, a fact that eases the gnawing suspicion of my own bad faith, helping me to believe that more than personal vengeance was involved and affording me the illusion of having reestablished, if not justice, at least a kind of balance, a natural compensation. But surely there must be some lesson in all this—one I hope to understand before I die.

What follows is the tale I told Hans, a story I carried within myself for more than forty years. It concerns a man I lost track of just after the war but never gave up looking for. I refrain from mentioning his name only out of regard for others in this country who might share it, men who, I believe, live in justice and have nothing to do with him.

It is, in the first place, the story of a rivalry played out on a chessboard, that array of squares which seems small only to those unable or unwilling to grasp its depth, for it is, in fact, a world unlimited and not at all innocuous. What occurs on it, in the form of a creative act sometimes resembling a true work of art, is in reality a struggle of exceptional violence, a form of bloodless homicide whose outcome is shared by the contenders alone. Nothing binds two people like a serious challenge on a chessboard, making them counterposed poles of a jointly produced mental creation in which one is annihilated to the other's advantage. There is no harsher or more implacable defeat. The players bear lifelong scars, neither body nor soul ever recovering fully. Anything that might reawaken memory of the mutilation is violently repulsed.

It was exactly this awareness that drove me so incessantly in my search for this man. For years I attended every major tournament in Europe, seeking out anything related to the game in any way, compiling a vast archive. But there was never any trace of him.

My hope of eventually tracking him down rested on the conviction that however much time might pass, I would recognize him beneath any change of identity and any disguise, even if his features had been altered by a surgeon's scalpel. Nevertheless, I often came close to giving up. I wondered what had become of him. Where could he be? I knew I'd never find him outside the world of chess, but I had no real fear he might have abandoned the game. A player like him never quits completely. Even if he decides not to participate in tournaments and competitions, he will still maintain some connection, through games by correspondence, through study and analysis, perhaps even by becoming a respected scholar, writing books and articles on chess theory.

There remained the remote possibility that he'd died, thus vitiating my quest. But the constant sensation of a looming threat convinced me that both of us were still in this world.

At first I didn't tell Hans about this man. I knew that in time I would, however things worked out, but for the moment he had only to play in my stead. Any other thought would have been a distraction, and I had no wish to complicate the training I'd forced upon him. His risky, combative style made him the ideal executor of my strategy, the person who could implement my variation in active play. The chess world, ever avid for novelty, would seize upon it, subjecting it to the most meticulous analysis, such that even if it was demolished, it would surely be noticed, most of all by the man who already knew it so well, having experienced it personally.

What I am about to relate, however, is a story not merely of earthly rivalry but of *adversity,* a term that conveys the proper sense of an irresistible force set in motion by an intelligence capable not only of bringing about ineluctable events but also of subverting all human principles so as to instill within us, in an act of the most extreme oppression, first the suspicion and eventually the certainty that we ourselves, along with the Divinity that rules us, are the sole existing evil.

I say this because I am convinced that the story transcends the purely personal domain. Certain as I am that even phenomena of truly vast proportions can be traced back to an infinitesimal starting point, there are times, in my most gloomy reflections, when I feel that the ultimate origin of the implacable chain reaction that soon engulfed the world lay here, in the sumptuous Hotel Friedrichsbad, on the day the two of us first met over a chessboard as mere adolescents.

Were I asked when I learned to play chess, I would not know how to reply. I feel as though I've always played, in the most remote times and places. What I had to learn, if anything, was the rules of this century and this planet.

Nevertheless, for me the game is bound inextricably to my father, or rather, to something that stood behind him like a projection of the past, a conscious and calculating ghost.

My father was nearly fifty when I was born. I was an only child, and he was a stern parent. I found momentary refuge only in my mother's affection, and only with her complicity was I allowed to play the games played by children my own age, which my father considered vain and harmful. He believed that everything I did must have a formative, pedagogical intent. However wide I cast my memory, I recall no moment of joy or frivolity not accompanied by a sense of guilt. My father held that every failing, however slight, deserved punishment. But the penalty had to be inflicted without anger or resentment, on the contrary requiring tranquillity and serenity, like therapy. In this regard I retain a most singular memory of him. He punished my disobedience with an old belt, a fairly common practice in those days. But he applied it in a special way. He didn't punish me at once, nor did he tell me when it would happen. Instead he let me wonder indefinitely, until some evening, after dinner, the reply to my questions would arrive as I headed down the hallway on my way to bed: at the bottom of a glass basin filled to the brim with water and placed in plain sight on a washstand, I would see my father's belt, coiled like a black snake. That was my notice. The threat would hang over me for days or weeks, until my debt was judged to have overflowed. Only then was the admittedly infrequent penalty administered, rapidly and when I least expected it. Sometimes he would wake me in the middle of the night to settle accounts, belt in hand.

In my mind my father was the corporeal, terrestrial embodiment of a boundless spiritual hierarchy, first rung of our faith, tangible representative of the ineffable and terrifying Supreme Being who always expected my most absolute devotion and obedience.

A modern sociologist might argue that my talent for chess was rooted in my early childhood environment, but I prefer to think that it existed beforehand and was simply drawn to the person, or the world, that offered it the best chance to unfold. However that may be, the fact is that my father, too, had a passion for chess, and had been a formidable player in his youth. He claimed that Chigorin himself had been his friend and master. By the time I was born, his age and many commitments kept him from playing, but the passion was still intact.

My father was a wealthy art dealer who traveled constantly, and once I learned to move the pieces, he began taking me with him on his trips, during which I had the opportunity to attend major tournaments and follow the games of the great champions of the era. Usually he would pick one of the most interesting contests, and we would watch the display board on which the game was presented to the audience. Chess was a language I understood from my earliest years. It was like being present at a natural event, like admiring the sky or the sun, whose beneficent existence brooked no question or challenge. But my father had no idea I felt this way. He thought I was just a quiet, well-behaved boy who could stand beside him for hours with no sign of impatience.

A formidable group of players was touring Europe and America at the time, a kind of itinerant Olympic team headed by the Cuban Capablanca, who seemed impregnable after taking the world championship from Lasker.

Among the great champions of the day was one who aroused my father's particular admiration. His name was Akiba Rubinstein, one of the greatest players of all time. Though the frailty of his nerves prevented him from attaining absolute supremacy, his play was held to be matchless, and my father did whatever he could never to miss a tournament in which Rubinstein played. He would suddenly rush off on what he claimed was an urgent business trip. He and I alone knew that the journey just happened to coincide with a competition in one of the cities on our itinerary. A sale of precious porcelain was being held in Prague? Yes, but Rubinstein was playing there as well. An important auction had been scheduled in London? True, but on the way we would stop in a town where, as if by chance, Rubinstein, too, was present. I have often wondered whether my father's unbounded admiration for this man stemmed solely from his play or whether it was partly because they shared the same surname (Tabori, which I adopted after the war, was my mother's maiden name) and because both had their roots in the eastern ghetto. What is certain is that mere mention of his name seemed to rejuvenate my father. When he replayed one of Rubinstein's games, his face would assume a strangely harsh expression of repressed excitement, similar to the one I saw when he lingered at a painting or listened to music.

One day I asked my father to teach me to play chess, a suggestion he'd never made himself. Not that he'd forbidden me to touch the pieces, but neither had he done anything to fire my passion until I spontaneously asked him to be my teacher. (Perhaps that was what he was waiting for.) I must have been six or seven. In reality, as I said, I already knew nearly everything about the game. Only a few rules, such as how to capture en passant or how to castle, were less than fully clear to me. My father got a board and set to beginning a game with me, obviously expecting to have to explain things as we went along. But his expression soon shifted from amusement to surprise, perplexity, and outright concern. Almost without realizing it, he found himself in difficulty. He refused to believe that my moves were guided by chance alone, and from time to time he stared strangely at me over the frame of his eyeglasses. His optimistic attack collapsed miserably. He was forced to cede a pawn, then a knight. Finally, realizing he would lose if the game continued, he called a halt and put the board away.

A few days later he took me to a little room off his study that had been kept under lock and key for years, he alone being permitted to enter. Driven by my child's curiosity, during his absences I had often tried to pick the lock to find out what might be hidden there, and I was stunned and dismayed that he was now bringing me in. I thought I was going to be punished for some misdeed, perhaps for having tried to penetrate the threshold I was about to cross. So I was trembling with fear and excitement when, once inside, he had me sit down at a chessboard that stood gleaming on a pedestal in the half shadows of the empty room, a board unlike any I'd ever seen. At that point my father told me he would be my master, as his father had been his and his grandfather had been his father's before him. Chess, he said, had been handed down through the generations in our family. It was believed that this chain— along with a threat of horrible curses on whosoever might break it—had begun with a merchant ancestor in the early seventeenth century. Having encountered Joachim Greco on his return from a journey to the Orient, this merchant had played chess for, and lost, a shipment of precious Shiraz jewels. According to the story, my ancestor decided that the firstborn son of every generation of his issue should excel in this game. I never found out whether this story was wholly invented or contained a grain of truth. Perhaps the flourish about a material loss was added to make the tale more plausible to my child's mind, but I always suspected that something else was hidden behind it, something my father would someday reveal to me if I did not eventually discover it for myself.

The board in my father's room was so strange it seemed to have come from another world. Or perhaps it was a sacred object. Inscribed on one side were the twenty-two letters of the Hebrew alphabet. On the other three sides, half erased by time, were sayings my father claimed to have deciphered: "Thou shalt not cause pain. Thou shalt flee pain. Thou shalt learn from pain." They sounded like commandments or an indecipherable prophecy. He also told me that this board had extraordinary power: it would punish error instantly, acting on the unconscious accumulation of negative energy that inevitably accompanies any infringement of harmony. It would be ineffective only on the mind of a madman or the superhuman loneliness of genius, and it was by subjecting me to that test (from which I emerged unscathed) that he first suspected that I was the culmination of the experiences transmitted to us by the past.

But he also had to find out whether I had genuine natural talent. I seemed to be able to subvert the rules of the game as a juggler seems to subvert the laws of gravity, creating the strangest and most paradoxical complications. The truth is that I was enamored of risk and especially enjoyed snatching victory from apparently hopeless positions.

My father insisted that my exuberance had to be checked and controlled by discipline and methodical study. I had no idea what was in store for me when I asked him to teach me to play, and at times I came to hate the game I so loved, for the practice and study he imposed were pure torture. He was an inflexible master, forcing me to practice for hours as you would practice a musical instrument, perfection always just out of reach. God knows I would have loved to play even a single game for pure amusement, as my classmates did. I would have loved to feel the game's playful side just for an instant. But this was denied to me from the outset. My father informed me that the worship of chess, and in particular its rigor, had been handed down for generations in our family and could never be ignored.

He was my first and only master, stern and unbending. He made me promise never to play with anyone but him. He took me only to the most important tournaments, telling me to pick a player and to try to predict his moves. I don't deny that it was an excellent exercise, and rarely did I err. Often I would have ventured more brilliant variations, but unfortunately I was not yet the one moving pieces on the board.

During this time, between the ages of nine and twelve, I discovered a kind of clairvoyant gift that enabled me to discern just how deep was any given player's bondage to the game. It appeared to me in the form of a luminous star-shaped spot, almost a brand, in the center of the forehead, a laceration barely perceptible in some but cryingly obvious in those totally dominated by their passion for the game, those fated to find fulfillment or annihilation in it, experiencing it as an earthly expiation or a life sentence. The spot, as fleeting as a jack-o'-lantern's flame, appeared independent of my will and only in special conditions of indirect lighting (most easily in half shadow). The gift vanished completely when I turned thirteen and returned only once, some ten years later, in most unusual circumstances.

My father was well known in the chess world. His enthusiasm often extended to patronage, and several famous champions became family friends. Chess players would visit our house in Munich, and wherever players gather, the talk is of one thing only. Comments about this or that game soon led to demonstrations on the board, and by now I could express opinions of my own, for the game had yielded its secrets to me, and even though my father had been my sole opponent, my judgments were not only heeded but usually proved correct. It filled me with pride that my father treated me like an adult in these gatherings, letting me stay up late if I wanted. And he warned the others with the utmost seriousness that they would have to deal with me in due course.

There was a period when the great champions of the day were regular visitors. Vidmar, Tartakover, Znosko Borovski, the corpulent Bogoliubov (considered the unofficial challenger for the world title) are among the ones I remember. Vidmar was a well-mannered, taciturn man, a frugal eater who treated his stomach with the same respect as he did the game, while Znosko and Bogo were insatiable, florid, and boisterous, with a passion for vodka and beer, respectively. Tartakover, in contrast, was a perfect gentleman and an excellent pianist who also did magic tricks that left me dazzled.

To me chess seemed a world populated by heroes and invincible warriors, but there came a day when I glimpsed just how unsteady were the pillars on which it rested. I realized then that some gleaming mental constructions contain within them, concealed by the thinnest of shells, a hollow world ever on the brink of collapse, threatening to engulf everything in its ruin.

In biographies of the great players of the past I had read of the madness, sometimes harmless, sometimes violent, that marked the lives of some chess geniuses. I knew of the leaden depression into which the great Morphy had fallen, of Pillsbury's horrible death at such a young age, of the delusions of grandeur that overpowered Steinitz's limpid mind in the last years of his life. Yet when we know of such things only through books, we tend not to grasp that illness, pain, and madness are not always and everywhere the same, for they rage even more terribly when their victim is a genius.

I will never forget the evening Akiba Rubinstein came to our house—for us an exhilarating event. It was Tartakover who brought him, after years of urging by my father. On his return from a recent success in Budapest, Rubinstein had competed in an important tournament in Karlsbad, placing third among twenty-three, behind Nimzovitch and Capablanca. There was no doubt he was still a great player. My father spent weeks looking forward to the evening and days racked by doubt as to whether Rubinstein would show up. We knew that he had neither friends nor relatives and was not in the best of health. Tartakover had taken him to the hotel he was staying at in Munich, paying out of his own pocket after finding Rubinstein wandering aimlessly near the train station, penniless and with no place to go, complaining that someone had robbed him on the train. We also knew he had no love for Bogoliubov and several other players, whom my father had been careful not to invite. I myself had been given detailed instructions. I was not to stare at him or speak to him, injunctions that naturally inflamed my already lively curiosity.

We waited for a long time and sat down to eat after eventually losing hope that he would ever arrive. Just then a taxi pulled up, and Rubinstein, accompanied by Tartakover, entered without a word, merely nodding briefly at us. At first he refused to take off his coat, in the end reluctantly agreeing to consign it to a servant. Before he sat down he wiped the seat of his chair with a handkerchief. Though we'd attended many of his games, I'd never seen him so close up. He was a small man, portly now, with eyeglasses, a waxed mustache, and thinning hair carefully arranged over his high forehead.

Someone felt duty-bound to congratulate him on his most recent success. He greeted the brief applause with a grimace of satisfaction, but then immediately began wiping dishes and silverware with the handkerchief balled up in his hand—a seemingly pointless exercise, since he took only a few mouthfuls of each dish served to him, pushing the food around his plate with a fork as though looking for something. He was no less sparing in his speech, uttering no more than a word or two in more than an hour. Yet this was Rubinstein, "the player no mortal could equal," sitting right there in front of me.

The others continued to converse quietly among themselves, but everyone felt awkward. Inevitably the talk turned to chess, a subject that ought to have interested our honored guest. But perhaps he was too absorbed by the game to want to talk about it.

It was already midnight. The barely perceptible tolling of a grandfather clock in the salon could be heard just as Rubinstein's glass tipped over on the table. This seemed to rouse him from his torpor, and everyone else fell silent. But the phrase he uttered had nothing to do with what they'd been talking about. It seemed to come bubbling to the surface from somewhere in the depths of him, and it was a phrase that chilled us, for it sounded like a plea for help.

"Someone's knocking," he said in a falsetto voice. "They never give me a moment's peace, there's never an end to this torment, they knock on the walls of my room day and night."

He then sank back into himself. For the rest of the evening he never said a word, never ate a bite, never drank. He sat nailed to his seat, staring at his hands.

His face was lit by the soft lighting, and behind him were bare walls. These were ideal conditions for awakening my faculties, and as I looked at Rubinstein's forehead, I clearly perceived the dimensions the laceration had assumed in him. It seemed to have invaded his entire brow, its edges visible only in a faint and fragile jagged line.

I had no way of knowing that the tournament he had just played in would be his last. He was now condemned beyond appeal. An irreversible catatonia had gripped him.

Soon it was time for my debut, which occurred in 1929 in a most unexpected way, aboard the *Bremen,* a steamer taking us from Europe to New York. During the first days of the voyage my father told me he had a surprise for me, and one evening he led me into the reception hall, where many small tables with fine chessboards had been arranged in a circle. José Raúl Capablanca was to play an exhibition of twenty-five simultaneous games, and my name was listed among his opponents, who included more than a few known masters.

My excitement at the prospect of playing the legendary Capablanca more than compensated for all the sacrifices I'd made. I earned a stalemate by forced repetition at the twenty-ninth move. Only three of us—two noted masters and myself—managed to draw, the others losing in just a few moves. I was still a mere boy, and Capablanca shook my hand and predicted a brilliant future for me.

In those days all chess fans were anxiously following the interminable negotiations for a world-title rematch. After dominating the scene for more than twenty years, Capablanca had finally been upset by the rising star of Alexander Alekhine. He was now eager for revenge. Two years had gone by, but nothing had been set. The Russian seemed in no hurry, finding countless excuses to postpone a rematch. Certainly the exhausting battle with the Cuban, which had lasted seventy-four days, was still fresh in his memory.

The single defeat had robbed the ex-champion of none of his greatness. He continued to participate in international tournaments, winning one victory after another. It was thanks to him that chess gained followers in increasing numbers. Everyone was eager to learn. It was a golden age, almost as though people were desperate to be distracted from an unsettling future. Only forty years later, with the emergence of the irrepressible Bobby Fischer, was there a comparable period. Every city seemed to hold at least one annual tournament, and the hefty purses put up by patrons (my father among them) drew all the top names. Publishers, too, were eager for works on chess. Classics were reissued and countless manuals published, as well as collections of games and records of tournaments. Every daily newspaper had a chess column that reported major games and printed endless diatribes by players of opposing factions, as well as letters from readers intent on having their say about this or that event. There was much debate about whether chess required mere cunning and intelligence or whether, as in other art forms, inspiration was also needed. Alekhine himself seemed intent on dividing the chess world into two distinct blocs: genuine artists versus athletes who aimed solely at winning by any means necessary, to the detriment of the game itself.

This was the world I was about to enter, with the tacit promise that I would soon be competing with great champions and would one day aspire to the world title.

After such a brilliant debut, I'd expected that on our return from America I would begin playing in qualification tournaments immediately. But things didn't go as I'd thought. A theatrical impresario who organized minor shows and stunts in village venues convinced my father—or rather, successfully appealed to his unbounded vanity—to send me out on simultaneous exhibitions of up to twenty-five games. I was only eleven years old and did not look at all aggressive or even particularly intelligent. People who expected to play against a bearded old man with a wrinkled brow were flabbergasted to find that their opponent was a little boy in short pants. My appearance was often greeted with gales of incredulous, scornful laughter. My opponents were almost always adults, sometimes prominent personalities or aristocrats, but their view of the game was so parochial that I was able to outplay them with little difficulty. I admit I found it amusing. I enjoyed watching them stumble, flounder, lose patience, and finally become angry. Generally they couldn't believe their eyes even when facing incontestable defeat, but ultimately they had no choice but to bow to the evidence: I was the superior player. Some tried to justify their defeat by claiming to have lost on purpose so as not to hurt my feelings. Others accused me of cheating (as if it were possible to cheat at chess), hinting that moves had been secretly communicated to me by a master concealed in the hall. Still others claimed that I hypnotized my opponents, that I read their minds, that I was possessed by the Devil. Some suggested—and this rumor spread with impressive speed—that I was not eleven but thirty, a dwarf disguised as a child. In short, they took me for a con man and treated me with corresponding disdain. "A Little Jew's Stunt" was one newspaper's headline about me. From then on, it was regularly mentioned that I was Hebrew, a word that embodied all possible slanders.

It was during this period that I met him for the first time, at one of my exhibitions. I believe that somewhere in the world each of us has his own antagonist, his negative alter ego, like he who stands against the Holy Names of the Tree of Life, the *Qlippah,* whose name wise men urge us not even to utter, the serpent ever ready to raise his head, the adversary we hope never to encounter but whom we inevitably come upon in the end, for he is part of our very being. In my case it was as though all the centuries of struggle by past generations were aimed solely at preparing this mortal conflict.

I met my fated adversary in Baden-Baden, during a simultaneous exhibition at the Hotel Friedrichsbad. I hope I don't sound smug when I say that he had human features. Among my many opponents was a boy, the last to arrive, who looked two or three years older than me. He was introduced with the title of baron, and he, too, was accompanied by a proud father.

On his forehead I immediately noticed the mark of a hopeless chess worshipper. I also saw that he envied me, despised me. He was the only one to give me serious trouble that day, so much so that it was as though I were playing a single, exhausting game. I stepped along the circle of boards, making my moves on each, but my mind was focused only on his position.

He was the last of my opponents to remain, and luckily the game ended in a draw. His father dripped with pride. See? he seemed to say. Give him one more chance and my son'll teach that snotnose a lesson! His son's expression was no different. From the way he acted, many onlookers assumed he had won, and it was he who was hailed that night. An enthusiastic supporter introduced him to the audience as the true hope of chess, a future contender for the world title.

Very late that evening he made me a vow. He waited for me behind a curtain in a hallway, and as I walked by on my way to my room, he pushed me against a wall, held his fist in my face, and hissed, "You'll pay for this, Jew!" He was bigger and stronger than I, and I could not respond to his attack.

It was an incident I never forgot. I'd never been seriously threatened before, and from then on I was certain I would encounter him in my path.

When the contract with the impresario expired, my father began entering me in qualification tournaments. At twelve I was already a master, and by fourteen I'd earned a ranking that today would be called international grand master. The tournaments became ever more competitive. Whereas earlier I was always the uncontested victor, I now faced ever rising difficulties. Nevertheless, I regularly finished among the leaders and won the right to compete against top players, despite my youth.

In those first years the presence of my chosen adversary was a constant torment to me. He turned up in every tournament, and though fate seemed to spare us direct conflict, almost as if deliberately postponing it to a more propitious occasion, I always had the feeling I was playing against him and him alone. We were antagonists at a distance. Our eyes would meet across a room full of roiling chessboards, and since the rules permitted us to stroll around while our opponents pondered their moves, I'd sometimes sense him behind me. And he must have sensed me, too.

He struck a kind of dread in me. Yet I had no doubt which of us was the better player. I knew his style and had analyzed several of his games, finding nothing original in them. He was a conservative player, still bound to the schematic methods of Tarrasch (the grand old man of chess in Germany), not at all influenced by the hypermodern theories then fashionable. Yet it was precisely his lack of originality, risk, and imagination, his slavish adherence to dogma, that made me so uneasy.

He also won a number of matches against players of some ranking and finished among the leaders in several tournaments. At first I wondered how, but what counts in chess is not only the play but the attitude of the players. Old chess manuals were full of advice about how to irritate your adversary, maneuvering him into an inferior position even before the game begins. There were countless examples of such tactics, from Lasker's pestilential cigar to Steinitz's foul language.

The threats he'd made against me the evening of our first encounter were indelible in my memory. I knew that when the time came for us to face each other over the board I would have to protect myself against his very presence more than against his play. I would have to bear up under that presence for the entire duration of a tournament game.

Physically, too, we couldn't have been more different. I was small and chubby; he was tall and very thin, like a stork in short pants. I had brown curly hair; his was blond, fine, and straight, falling over one temple. In short, I was a Jew and he an Aryan. The last time I saw him as an adolescent, in the Kaiserhof Café in Berlin, he was dressed in the uniform of the Hitler Youth, the representative, the chess hope, of the new race then asserting itself so resoundingly in Germany.

Although chess was my whole life in those days, it was also a perfect microcosm of a world that seemed poised on the brink of great events. The typical terms of the game—attack, mastery, conquest, victory—were being applied to a larger reality already undergoing dreadful changes. One day in May 1933 a huge bonfire was held in Berlin. The flames were fed by books: the works of Freud, Proust, and Einstein, but also of Steinitz, Nimzovitch, and Rubinstein. In the meantime, sales of *Mein Kampf* passed the one million mark. Orchestras were forbidden to perform works by Mendelssohn, Schönberg, and other Jewish composers. Sixteen thousand paintings, drawings, and sculptures representing what had been branded "degenerate art" were seized from galleries and exhibition halls and destroyed. Only thanks to the foresight of people like my father were many masterpieces saved from the conflagration. My father, indeed, was not merely an art dealer but also a true art lover, a man of modern, far-seeing ideas. Often he kept precious works for himself, flatly refusing to sell them. Among these was an entire collection of works by avant-garde painters. Only a handful of them were saved: the ones Hans admired on the walls of my apartment.

Soon an overt boycott of Jews was launched. They were barred from official duties, from universities, and from Parliament. By the end of 1933 tens of thousands had already decided to leave Germany. But many, paradoxically, saw positive signs in what was happening. Indeed, was not the coming of the Messiah to be inevitably preceded by terrible events? If so, it was a sad prophet indeed who now made his presence felt. Nevertheless, many still believed they could stay put even in the face of all the onerous restrictions. After all, they were Germans, were they not? Many were veterans of the Great War. They had fought for the fatherland, whose ideals and heroes they shared. It was "their" country, too, was it not? And if nothing on this earth was guaranteed, where else might a secure refuge lie?

If anything has characterized our race for millennia, it is a kind of fatalism or resignation. Granted, there were millions of us, but we were an immense flock ready to scatter at the mere appearance of a snarling dog. And Germany was the corral in which we were trapped, overtaken by a paralyzing panic. We returned to the life of the ghetto, to the fringes, while military parades and assemblies churned all around us and the air rang with loud, threatening voices. A meticulous selection was already under way. All men were required to add the name of Israel to their own, all women that of Sarah. Our citizenship was withdrawn, turning us into interlopers whose visas were about to expire. There was talk of moving us en masse to Madagascar or of sending us back to Palestine, which for many meant having to acknowledge their own historic failure. Where, then, was the longed-for Promised Land?

My father was among those who fell victim to the sin of optimism, despite what two thousand years of history should have taught him. His wealth gave him a sense of invulnerability that made him feel secure. He refused to flee when it was still possible to do so, instead merely withdrawing from the epicenter. We moved to Graz, in Austria, where we owned a house. Living conditions seemed more tolerable there.

In the midst of these tragic events, however, two men continued to seek each other out, like opposite electrical charges in a raging storm. I had gone away, but he came after me, and so it was that we met again, five years later, at the last tournament I was allowed to participate in. It happened in Vienna, late in the winter of 1938.

I recognized him immediately. He was now decked out in the radiant uniform of the SS, and his enmity was undiminished. He looked at me with scorn.

From the very first rounds it was clear he meant to let no one rob him of the prize, least of all me. For several days we were even in points, like two Alpinists striving to conquer the same peak from opposite slopes, each resolved to reach the top before the other. All signs were that we would clash directly in the final rounds, a climax I'd foreseen from the outset.

The tournament was held in a municipal building. Nearly all the participants, myself included, were lodged at the Hotel Krone, not one of the best inns, but willing to accommodate the schedule by keeping the restaurant open after midnight. Players, friends, supporters, and fans made for a steady flow of customers, but there was something sinister beneath the show of merriment, as though these people were lacking some essential thing I was unable to identify. Every face seemed to sport the same expression, as though one of the muscles required for the complex gesture of a smile had been severed, or the nerve controlling humor and irony, the satisfaction intelligence reserves to itself, had been cut.

I felt threatened. Granted, I'd been absent from the chess world for some time, but I didn't know a single player in that tournament, and soon enough I realized I would find no new friends among this group. One evening the subtle sense of danger suddenly took shape in a fleeting phrase overheard in the restaurant as I passed the table at which my adversary sat, attended by his court.

"These Jewish swine shouldn't be allowed to . . ." someone said, and the phrase could have been aimed at no one but me.

I sat in my usual place, still thinking about the game that had just ended. It was nine o'clock in the evening, and the room was packed. Songs and voices rose from the dinner party at the table nearby, and the bursts of laughter from that merry crew seemed to mock me.

Perhaps it was because I was the only one sitting alone in the large room, the only one silent while shards of scintillating Viennese conviviality poured down around me, but the sense of looming menace was suddenly stronger than ever. At bottom, I thought, it is within ourselves that madness takes root. All at once everything seems malevolent, without anything actually happening in the outside world. I tried to calm myself, telling myself that perhaps it was only my imagination, for I was young and impressionable.

More than an hour passed before anyone condescended to

serve me. After waving repeatedly at waiters who seemed blind and deaf, I finally managed to order dinner. Half an hour later I was informed that they'd run out of what I'd asked for. I ordered something else; the ultrapolite waiter carefully noted it down. But was he really a waiter, or the scribe who takes the names of souls cast onto the banks of the river of death?

At that instant I suddenly remembered Rubinstein and saw him sinking into his own spiral of madness in the most complete and dismayed impotence. His shrill, terrible voice rang in my ears: "They never give me a moment's peace . . . they knock on the walls of my room day and night." And in a flash I understood the sinister foreboding of those words.

In the meantime the revelry at my antagonist's table continued. Champagne corks popped, and the chain of toasts seemed endless.

Now in despair, I managed to get the waiter's attention.

"Sorry, sir, but we're all out of everything," he said in dismay.

Naturally I protested.

"I'll go see if there's anything left in the kitchen," he said.

This time I didn't have long to wait. The hotel manager himself approached my table, followed by a waiter pushing a cart laden with a large covered platter. Their arrival did not pass unnoticed. Many fell silent. When they reached my table, the waiter raised the silver lid with a flourish and placed the severed head of a baby goat before me.

"I'm afraid this is all we have," he said. They both walked away before I could recover from my horror and disgust.

A roar of laughter rose from that dinner party. The company

raised their glasses to me in a toast wholly innocent of good wishes.

Only then did I realize that I'd been the target of an elaborate cruel joke. I looked around and saw that everyone in the restaurant, even those sitting farthest from me, had been part of it, though they were careful not to show it. I was treated to stares of ironic commiseration, while they exchanged glances of complicity among themselves. People leaned with affected nonchalance to whisper to their companions, who in turn repeated the identical gesture, until the persistent pantomime, meant to be unobserved, finally became too obvious. Heads leaned one upon the other like bowling pins. A shudder of hilarity spread through the room. Exiting was the most difficult part. I left the dining room in a hail of insults.

A warning like this should have put me on guard. Anyone with any common sense would have packed his bags and gone home. But there was still chess, and chess was my sole reason for living.

As I'd foreseen from the start, at nine the next morning we were matched in the final, decisive game. We were even in points. Whoever won this game would win the tournament. I arrived on time and took my seat. There was no sign of my adversary. He had the first move, and the referee started his clock. The distressing wait lasted for more than fifteen minutes, not an inconsequential period, and the time was charged against him. But the ticking of the clock soon sounded like hammering, a symbolic embodiment of his disquieting presence. Chess players tend to be nervous people: they expect everything to go as planned and are upset by any hitch. This delay irritated me, and since I suspected it was deliberate, it struck me as an unpardonable lack of respect. Nor was I cheered by the knowledge that in another fifteen minutes I would win by forfeit.

Finally he arrived, not in any hurry. He sat down. Before making his opening move, he placed a one-pfennig coin beside the board. "I never play without a stake," he said. And tense as I was, I had to rummage in my pocket for a coin of equivalent value. I was playing his game before we even started.

He opened with his queen's pawn, setting up a positional game not at all congenial to me. Our pieces were soon so cramped as to permit no initiative. On about the thirtieth move I tried to break the logjam by sacrificing two pawns, gaining some breathing room and launching a long-range combination that eventually re-created a situation of absolute parity, albeit through unexpected pathways. I realized I would rather lose than continue this way. The game was adjourned on the fortieth move. I spent the rest of the morning analyzing it, but failed to come up with anything. Play resumed that afternoon and continued till late in the evening. It was the last game still in progress, and the others gathered around us. But the contest continued as it had begun, lifeless and placid. As I'd feared, it ended in a draw: neither of us had any way to win. The match would therefore be decided by tallying the scores of our previous opponents. Since these figures were clearly in my favor, I had no doubt that I'd won.

But the referees seemed unable to agree. After long and heated debate, they retired like a panel of judges deliberating a difficult case, and finally it was announced that he was the winner. I was not listed as second, or as third, or as last. When

I protested vigorously, no one listened. In the end someone was kind enough to tell me that I'd been disqualified for improper play. I was then virtually ejected from the hall.

And that was not the end of the surprises. On returning to the hotel, I found my room ransacked, my suitcases and closets emptied, my belongings scattered on the floor. The photographs of my parents, which I carried with me everywhere, were torn and spattered, the frames trampled. My clothing and personal effects had been trampled as well.

I sank into a chair, on the edge of panic. There were footsteps in the hallway, and I heard a knock at the door. It was the innkeeper, and he, too, seemed upset. He advised me to leave as quickly as possible; otherwise "they" would come back and set fire to the hotel. I was so flustered I barely grasped what he was saying. All I understood was that I was being evicted. A car was waiting for me at the service entrance. I stuffed my things into a suitcase and hurried out.

As the taxi took me through the city to the station, I felt as though I'd been dropped onto another planet, a cruel and hostile place. Inclined by character to silence and reflection, I'd always been repulsed by noise and uproar, by any manifestation of the excessive merriment that so often borders on violence. I'd always detested student revelry, as though death became even more menacing to me precisely in the rites meant to exorcise it. But at that moment I felt only fear. The streets of Vienna were home to an obscene festival. There were piles of broken furniture everywhere. People lurched along the sidewalks as though drunk. There were shouts and curses, and here and there the crack of isolated shots. So many streetlamps along Argentinierstrasse had been shattered that long tracts of the roadway were in darkness. When the taxi arrived at the station, a group of people surged up out of nowhere, trying to hem us in. The driver stomped on the gas pedal, and we barely missed them. They pounded the sides of the car as we passed. I could almost touch their menacing, or perhaps merely terrorized, faces. They ran after us, waving their arms. Rioting had broken out at Franz Josef Station as well. A crowd of curious onlookers had gathered on the square in front of the station to view a horrible spectacle: four people, kicking and spitting, were forcing an old man to crawl along the pavement, his clothing torn, a sign hanging from his neck.

I told the driver to go on to the next station, and here, too, there were scenes of violence. A manhunt was under way throughout Vienna. The crowds shouted, *"Juden, Juden raus!"*

But the person who most fully embodied the explosive hatred and repressed rancor of the man in the street for the Jews was the driver himself, who, apparently not suspecting that I was one of them, spewed scorn for the "cursed race" that had to be "wiped off the face of the earth." The livid nape of his coachman's neck, legacy of his father or perhaps of a hackney-driving grandfather, bulged between the collar of his leather jacket and the back rim of his shabby cap, expressing a dull-witted and implacable hostility, the very image of intolerance, like a hideous face in which every feature is scarred, dissolved in an unformed mass.

I was perhaps the last person in Vienna to realize that the rabid dog had bounded onto Austrian soil and that this first act of violence toward the neighboring nation had unleashed the worst instincts slumbering in the tranquil soul of the Viennese citizenry. The peaceful Kobold had been supplanted by a bloodthirsty Troll. Austria was gripped by an anti-Semitic hysteria that led to stunning outrages of violence. More than five hundred Jews lost their lives in Vienna alone that night and in the days that followed. Thousands more were deported to the first concentration camp, in Dachau.

Exactly eight months later another wave of violence was unleashed, on a vaster and even more vicious scale. One hundred and ninety-five synagogues were burned in Germany and Austria on the night of November 9–10, 1938. Thousands of shops belonging to Jewish families were looted and set ablaze, along with countless homes. At least twenty thousand people were arrested and deported to concentration camps. That night would forever be known as Kristallnacht, the Night of Broken Glass, an exquisitely poetic name for the start of a slaughter that was to have no end.

The Jews were soon deprived of all their rights. They had to wear a yellow star of David sewn to their clothes, a designation that barred them from frequenting public places or taking a stroll or looking in shop windows—in short, from living. In all the occupied territories chess, too, donned the brown uniform. Most well-known players disappeared, their names vanishing from the chess columns. Even the manuals were purged. Jewish players were mentioned only in the humor section, where their worst games and greatest blunders were recorded. The annals of the game must have been gone over with a fine-tooth comb to uncover such tasty tidbits.

Alongside the many unknown names that suddenly emerged out of nowhere, there was talk only of Alekhine and of his continuing efforts to postpone the rematch with Capablanca, a contest that never took place; the latter died unexpectedly in 1947. But anti-Semitic articles appeared with increasing frequency under the byline of the world champion, who railed at those who had brought the "noble game" so low and noted that after having been so long polluted by Jewish blood, the world of chess would also finally recover its purity.

My chess career naturally came to an end with the triumph of Nazism and the outbreak of the war. I was barred from tournaments and would not even risk playing a game in a coffeehouse or watching others play, partly because any public place (assuming there had been one willing to let me in) would have been a trap in the event of a raid. On the occasional Sunday, if the weather was good, I allowed myself the luxury of observing games played on large outdoor boards in the park. I would sit inconspicuously on a bench, my collar turned to conceal the yellow star, ready to vanish at the first sign of danger.

My parents and I lived in these conditions of nonexistence for some time, adjusting to restrictions whose number and ferocity mounted daily. We tried to stay out of sight as much as possible, rarely venturing out and whispering even at home when we talked among ourselves. We were sustained by the illusion that the many horrible things we heard concerned others remote from us and surely guilty of some grave offense if they were being punished so harshly. No such things would happen to us, who had done nothing wrong. We told ourselves that this, too, would pass. All we needed was the strength to endure it. But we were wrong. It meant nothing that some of us had so far been spared. Even an hourglass has its last grains of sand. And when finally it happened on our own street, when the people across the road and the neighbors on the floor below were taken away in the middle of the night, we realized that there was no hope, that surely our names also were already listed on a document awaiting a mere signature. We wrapped all our valuables in a roll of cloth and hid them under the floorboards of the attic of our house in Graz. Whoever of us survived could come back for them.

I have a vague, nebulous memory of that long, almost miraculous period of respite. It was a time of incessant wandering from village to village, of constant moves to new refuges, with ever new identities and documents but the same, unchanging fear. My father's money bought us much support, and we were generously aided by friends, Jews and non-Jews alike. But denunciation by a single person, betrayal by just one piece, was enough to do us in.

That was how the nightmare began. It was a waking nightmare, but as impossible to interrupt or modify as a dream. Overnight we were stripped of what little remained of our dignity, deprived of every human attribute. We spoke the same language as they did and expressed the same concepts, born of like feelings and needs, but the presumed equivalence was illusory, for they reduced us to the status of beasts of burden and animals for slaughter.

To this day I sometimes wonder—and it is *their* salvation I have in mind—whether all the people who participated so zealously in this vile task heard human voices rising from our ranks or whether, by some spell cast on their brains by their leaders' propaganda, they perceived only bleats and bellows.

We were herded and driven like animals, kept in line with

clubs, packed into cattle cars (where else?). The doors slid shut, leaving us in darkness, without air or food throughout the interminable journey. We had to squeeze against one another to fit into the space, to let the glimmer of light reach us, to shun the fetid stench of excrement and the horror of the first deaths. The only air filtered in from gratings too high up, vanishing completely when the train stopped for long hours in the sun. Only the lifeless bodies of the weakest, serving as supports, prevented others from suffocating.

I lost sight of my parents when the train set out. I was sure they were in the same convoy, but I despaired of ever finding them alive. When we arrived at our destination after several days and nights and the doors of the cars were opened, we were greeted by armed guards with dogs. Our first order was to remove the dead, stacking the corpses on the platform. Dozens and dozens had died in the cattle cars, mainly the old and the sick. Only then did I see my parents, but it was impossible to get near them. It was here, after an hour's wait, that the first selection took place. We were divided into four columns—women, men, old people, and children—and then marched to the camp. We had no idea how far it was, and many were too exhausted to walk. Those who stopped or fell were beaten, finished off on the spot if they were unable to go on. We were not allowed to help them in any way; we were forced to step over people who collapsed in front of us. Behind us we heard curses and the furious barking of dogs, followed by shots.

It took two endless hours to reach our destination, a collection of brick and wood buildings ringed by a ten-foot-high barbed-wire fence studded with guard towers and searchlights. Yet as we crossed an area as large as the small city it resembled, with blocks of freshly painted barracks and broad avenues intersecting at right angles, I felt a last, deceptive flash of comfort. I almost hoped that nothing bad could happen in such a scrupulously orderly place. There was even music: the notes of the *Tannhäuser* overture, coming from a phonograph, mingled with strains of Strauss waltzes played uncertainly by a grotesque group who stood on a wooden platform in the middle of the deserted square. But as we came nearer, we saw that the roof under which this little orchestra labored supported an immense beam from which jutted a series of hooks strong enough to hold a person's weight.

It was here that the various groups were separated. My mother seemed to follow her fate with resignation, lining up with the other women, holding in her arms a tiny bundle containing the few items she had with her. As they marched away, she raised a furtive hand to me in greeting, making a rapid, circular gesture, the palm of her hand held open, as though clearing a misted window to see me.

My father, on the other hand, refused to accept the affront. Suddenly he rebelled, protesting loudly and trying to move away from the group he was supposed to march with. Frozen with horror, I watched as they beat him with clubs and dragged him back. He fell, got up, groped for his lost eyeglasses. As he stooped, they hit him again, finally hurling him back among the others, unseeing, his face smeared with blood. It was the last time I saw my parents. Neither of them survived that place.

■　　■　　■

It isn't easy to speak of the days and months that followed. No detailed chronicle would ever succeed in conveying the depredations and systematic inner ravages to which we were subjected from the very first instant.

If it is true that the assertion of one's own individuality has always been a legitimate human aspiration, it is equally true that humanity has sought to cultivate scientific techniques for quashing this aspiration. One sure method of demolishing an individual's personality is to isolate him entirely from others, but a no less effective measure is to force him and his fellows into an inadequate space. In the former case the wellspring of madness appears centrifugal: absolute isolation tears consciousness from its moorings and sends it soaring into the giddiness of the infinite. But in a context of scarcity and enforced crowding consciousness also tends to lose its way, sliding into a centripetal madness that no longer looks to the future—or rather, to the panic of imminent disintegration—but instead turns in on itself, toward a prehuman past that crushes it under the unlikely sum of death and suffering that has already occurred. The personality regresses, dissolving into a common, instinctive soul in which nothing exists but the urge to withdraw from ubiquitous pain. If ever the spark of a different reaction might have displaced the utter feeble-mindedness into which we had been cast, it would perhaps have been generated, absurdly, by the very grotesqueness of the human condition. I imagined that reaction as a laugh that would suddenly engulf us all in a din terrible enough to shake the universe more than shrieks and weeping ever could.

But even the motive force we knew as pain began to fade in time, for only by becoming insensitive to all feeling could we hope to keep ourselves alive. There came a point when even pain ceased to grow, as when water in a sink reaches the safety drain, so that even though it continues to pour from the tap the level no longer rises. Feelings we'd once been proud of and believed to possess in abundance were annihilated. I was surprised to find that even hate itself was exhausted, slowly supplanted by a kind of absurd gratitude for the flickers of consideration we still aroused in them, enabling us to live through another day: the filthy pallets onto which we collapsed each night, the broth we were given to soothe the implacable hunger; after weeks of visceral torture, the hunger became a feeling of wrenching metaphysical solitude, as though every god had scorned us, condemned us forever and with no hope of appeal. In this condition of emptiness, abandonment, and betrayal, our persecutors rose to take the place of absent deities, for they possessed the power of life and death over us, a power they never hesitated to exercise. If they ordered someone to hang himself, the command was executed with vacant, robotic solicitude. One fashionable game they enjoyed when a jocular mood struck them was to snatch a prisoner's cap and toss it at the barbed-wire fence, across the demarcation line beyond which the guards had orders to shoot on sight. When instructed to go and fetch his cap, the prisoner would cross that line without a moment's vacillation, walking into death with absolute obedience. It was therefore not surprising that in time you began to feel a kind of admiration for the diligence with which they did their work, even beginning to worry whether you were perhaps too burdensome and eventually coming to feel guilty about it. This inner subversion, which in one sense was the most awful consequence of our captivity, long remained anchored in my being, like an impalpable feeling that I must not forget something I was nevertheless unable to remember. In later years I saw dozens of documentaries on the Nazi camps produced by the Reich's zealous moviemakers, but what had long been a mere sensation assumed the sharp contours of conscious memory in the form of a symbolic analogy, which caused me even greater suffering than my memory of the physical tortures. It happened as I watched a nature film. A herd of gazelles was attacked by predators and took flight, clustering in the savanna. One was caught and torn to pieces in the sunshine by the huge carnivores; the others watched the banquet from afar, and as the camera scanned their faces, filled with terror at their herdsmen-devourers, the definition I'd been seeking while unconsciously trying to avoid took sudden shape. In the gaze of those animals I saw our own, my own—frozen in fear, yes, but pervaded by what looked like ecstatic devotion.

The worst doubt about the Divinity that sometimes assailed me when I was a child was that behind His mask of wisdom and severity might lie a madman's face and that this might be the true countenance of the Father who made us in His image and likeness and to whom we swore eternal devotion. At times like that I could conquer my terror only by forcing my mind to cling to some familiar thing that belonged to me, focusing all my attention upon it until the blasphemous suspicion vanished.

But here in this alien world, where every human aspiration was eradicated and every divine principle subverted, where one false move brought massacre and life had value only so long as and insofar as it could be used as labor, everything around me became an abstraction. The dreams that supplanted reality at night eventually invaded my waking hours, becoming a continuous stream in which nothingness alone could account for nothingness. So it was that, paradoxically, the sole reality that kept me alive was an abstraction. What sustained me in that time without end was not the face of a loved one or a holy image but an enduring hallucination: a chessboard with flashing lights and shadows, rapid and evanescent.

Exactly when it happened I'm not sure. What I do know is that one day I began to play an interminable game. Whether it was my self or my God who sat across the board from me mattered little. That game soon took possession of all my thoughts. There was no space for anything else. It became my sole, irreplaceable faith.

True, the Torah warns us not to make idols of earthly things. But such rules were surely not meant for those who had been cast alive into Gehenna, as I was.

This thought never left me, even when I believed I was about to die. I later joined in an attempted escape, reluctantly, since I knew it would get us nowhere. We would remain at their mercy even beyond the barbed wire, and no one, neither we nor our executioners, would ever rise from the abject state into which the entire human race had fallen, even if we crossed those borders and lived another thousand years. Perhaps oblivion offered the sole possible release. Yet the primordial cell within us still obeyed the original, essential commandment of which life was presumably born and maintained: Thou shalt flee pain.

Once I'd passed the period of quarantine and been assigned to a work detail, all I did was dig. Exactly what we were digging we were never told. I was part of a squadron assigned to a tunnel, perhaps an underground shelter, at least half a mile from the camp. It was hard going, since the only effective tool we were given was an old jackhammer. Otherwise we had to make do with picks and shovels. After many weeks of labor we came upon a sort of natural underground vault that led, via a narrow passageway we could just about crawl through, beyond the hill and into the heath, out of range of the guard towers. Not suspecting there was another way out, our guards kept watch only on the entrance. They assumed that wherever we went in, there we would have to come out. The escape plan was to collapse the tunnel entrance and head for the unknown exit just before the end of work in the evening. Thinking we were trapped inside, the SS would waste time trying to dig us out. Once we were out of the tunnel we would scatter, hoping to fragment the forces of our pursuers at least temporarily. Though we had no idea where to go, we were convinced that no obstacle we might encounter in flight could be worse than what we had to endure every day.

With the complicity of the camp tailor we acquired uniforms that we patiently blackened with coal dust to look like civilian clothes, albeit of the worst possible cut, at least from a distance. Completely by accident, we picked a day that was particularly busy for the camp command. Two thousand new deportees had arrived, requiring the full mobilization of its organization.

It went off as planned, and we managed to escape. But I didn't get very far. The miner's lamp I had brought with me soon failed, and as I wandered the countryside in the dark, I stumbled into a deep hole, seriously injuring a leg. I struggled to make it to an abandoned hut. I spent the night in a sheep pen, but my leg was so swollen I was unable to stand.

At dawn I was awakened by the barking of dogs and a voice ordering me to come out with my hands up. I was taken back to the camp, where I saw they had recaptured all but one of us. But before I could rejoice about the one, I was told he'd been killed along the road. We were given an exemplary punishment. They wanted the other prisoners to see with their own eyes what would follow any attempt to flee the camp. Each of us was flogged, after which we were made to run in a circle on the Appellplatz, urged on by the kapos, whose rubber clubs (weapons that inflict great pain without breaking bones) ensured that no one missed a step. We ran that tragicomic carousel with signs hanging from our necks that read: "I love this place."

They had us run until we were exhausted. We looked truly ridiculous, myself most of all, as I was forced to hop on one foot. Incredibly enough, the sense of the ridiculous is the last thing we lose, and scorn and derision came even from the ranks of our fellow prisoners forced to observe the show, since our escape attempt would bring fresh torments for them as well.

That evening we were taken to the infirmary, where we were more or less put back together again for the rest of the punishment, which would continue until we lacked the strength to do any more than stand against the wall long enough to be shot. Not every escape attempt was punished by death, but since we'd collapsed the tunnel mouth, our crime included sabotage. The penalty for sabotage was execution by firing squad.

I was burning with fever by the time we were brought before the wall. My injured leg was infected, my body swollen and covered with bruises. But as I watched them form up in two ranks—one kneeling in front, the other standing in the rear—I thought again of chess, of the alignment of forces just before the first move. The ones kneeling were pawns, those standing were pieces. I pictured a gigantic invisible player about to make his opening move, and I was busily preparing my defense when they opened fire and everyone fell. I fell, too, beneath the bodies of the others, seeking to savor the moment of death, if ever that moment can have a taste no longer that of life.

But however hard I tried, I didn't quite manage to die. The fact that I could still feel myself and my surroundings, including the weight of bodies pressing down on me and voices howling above me, made me suspect that I was not yet dead—or that death was not a complete cessation of feeling. A succession of single shots began to ring out: the coups de grace were being administered. Soon it would be my turn, and that would surely put an end to all doubt, along with any capacity to feel doubt. At that moment I lost all awareness and believed I had died.

The visions I had in the state of unconsciousness into which I had fallen might well have convinced me that each of us has a heaven or hell tailored to our own measure. I don't know for how many days and nights I hallucinated an endless chess game, until one morning the awful figures that peopled my dreams took on human features.

I found myself back in the infirmary, stretched out on a straw pallet. A doctor and nurse stood beside me, observing my awakening with satisfaction. I was lying supine. I felt no pain. I touched myself and found no wounds. My leg had been carefully bandaged. Unbelievably, I was otherwise uninjured. Something or someone had halted my execution, but I had no reason to think it had been done for my own good. I don't know how long I remained in a half-sleeping, half-waking state. Eventually I sensed that my strength was returning, that my body was showing signs of life. Yet this place was often the final stopover before the ovens of the crematoria. Sanitation here was even worse than elsewhere, since many of the patients (forgive the absurd term) could not look after themselves. The crowding was beyond belief, two or even three people sometimes being put in the same bed. Illnesses spread instead of being eliminated, new maladies being contracted during treatments for old. There were countless cases of scarlet fever, measles, and typhus. Nearly everyone had some stage of dysentery. There was no water to drink or to wash with. The latrines were tin huts with a ditch underneath and two poles to sit on. At night we used iron tubs that were almost impossible to find in the pitch dark. Yet the white coats made their rounds in the midst of this decay, nurses and doctors visiting patients. The most startling contradiction was that these people, who strolled among the cots like haughty luminaries of medical science, stopping to chat with patients about their condition or the effects of treatment, might equally well decree death a moment later. In the infirmary it was almost always induced by an injection of formalin in the aorta, but execution was seldom performed on site. Patients considered incurable were dragged to a brick barracks behind the latrines. We called it the slaughterhouse. There they were left, sometimes for days after their instantaneous death. Selections were made almost daily, the unhappy chosen ones separated from the others and, so as not to dirty the beds, placed on waxed cloth, where they awaited their fate, perhaps for days on end, being given no food or water, since they were already listed as dead.

Yet here in this place I was now granted privileges: a double ration of potatoes and bread, real butter, even a cot all my own. My wounded leg had been treated and no longer hurt. I was told I'd escaped septicemia by a whisker.

One day a kapo ordered me to follow him to another section of the infirmary, where my clothes were taken and I was given a scorching shower. I was then taken to a barber, who cut my nails to the quick and shaved not only my beard and skull but my whole body, removing every hair. Next I was deloused and then subjected to a meticulous medical examination. Without excessive pain or bleeding a dentist extracted a molar he said was infected (assuring himself of his diagnosis by passing the tooth under his nose like the cork of a bottle of vintage wine). Finally my leg was rebandaged and I was issued a uniform, nearly new and freshly washed.

Now spick-and-span in my Sunday best, I was led by the kapo across the Appellplatz in the dazzling late September light. We went past the barracks to the camp headquarters, and to my great surprise we entered the building, passed through hallways and up staircases, and stopped at a door guarded by two SS men. Before the kapo opened it, he placed something in my palm as though it were a talisman. I clasped it tightly but had no time to figure out what it was, for I was pushed into a room. The door was closed behind me. I remained one step from the threshold, assuming the motionless stance required to avoid punishment, removing my cap and affecting the most humble demeanor I could muster, while nevertheless looking around surreptitiously. It was a fairly large room, its floor covered with rugs. Two banners, their black emblems vivid against red and white fields, hung on the wall to my right. Near a window at the far end, opposite the door I'd come in by, was a large desk. Behind the desk was a swivel armchair turned so that I could see only its tall back.

Just then a side door opened and a uniformed woman came in as though entering a stage from its wings. She went to the chair and leaned over to whisper something to the man presumably seated there, then turned and left as she had come. Only a few moments later did the armchair make a half turn to reveal its occupant.

The light was behind him. I couldn't make out his features and did not recognize him immediately. When he motioned me to approach, I crossed that boundless space with lowered eyes that dropped ever lower the closer I came. Trying not to damage the precious softness of the carpet with my clogs, I halted the requisite two paces from the desk. There was something familiar about the voice. "I have restored what was wrongly taken from you," it said. "Our last game ended in a draw, and I inadvertently pocketed your stake with my own."

I had no idea what he was talking about. My abnormal sense of guilt made me fear that a punishment far worse than death was now in store for me, but in a remote corner of my memory a spark of recognition glimmered without quite catching fire, and when the funereal awe I felt for that uniform faded, I saw the human features of a face in which, however hard I tried, I could detect nothing but the exquisite courtesy and elegance of manner that bespeak countless generations of good breeding. I was suddenly aware of the object I still held in my fist. It was a one-pfennig coin, and I was squeezing it so tightly it had nearly torn my flesh.

At exactly that moment the mark on his brow was revealed to me again, as if in a sinister epiphany.

It had been quite a few years, yet time had been kind to him. His skin was even clearer, his hair even finer. Though shaved at the neck and temples, he'd been permitted the affectation of a soft and flowing wave that nearly but not quite grazed his ear.

What honesty! was my blind and automatic response. To give me back my penny after all this time!

He had addressed me politely, treating me as his peer. Suddenly it seemed that everything I'd seen and suffered was only a bad joke, that life had all at once returned to normal.

"You may perhaps be wondering," he said, "to what you owe the succor that has come to you in such difficult straits. Well, I'll tell you. It has been my misfortune to find among my colleagues only lamentably inferior chess players. You are my only hope of being able to enjoy a few decent games. Surely you must be aware that we appreciate your merits and have sought to acknowledge your talents. You know, of course, that here in the camp we have a company of actors and an orchestra, clever craftsmen and carpenters, gardeners and cooks. I presume you would have no objection if in your case we seek to . . . cultivate . . . your talent for chess. All I ask is that you play a few games a week, for as long as I have the time and inclination. That will afford you, let us say, some extra chances. Now come and sit down!"

Only these final words were spoken in a tone of authority that brooked no refusal. He turned his back to the desk again. I took a step forward and noticed a small table with a chessboard already set up. There was also a stool. I realized that the stool was for me, and I took my seat without a word.

The pieces were of maple and ebony, smooth but not polished, of excellent quality, with an extraordinary balance of weight and form. The bases were padded with velvet that let them slide softly over the squares, on which they rested in a kind of haughty immobility.

We began to play, and the forgotten tactile-visual sensations, the simple gestures of moving the pieces over the board, gradually brought back a flood of memories of childhood and youth. I realized that my mental faculties were intact, that nothing had been lost, a discovery that was a bracing jolt to me. I was still a human being, with feelings and emotions. Sensations and memories churned in confusion, hurtling heavily toward the present, a time which until then had seemed unreal. Several times I had to fight back tears of self-pity that constricted my throat in an aching nostalgia for all I'd lost. The game continued almost independent of my will. Guided by a cold logic of their own, the white pieces worked their way among the black, opposing forces balanced each other, and far in the distance, like a flashing light, loomed the outlines of the final solution.

How long had it been since I'd played against a real opponent, pitting myself against a mind other than my own, with pieces I could actually touch and move? Years seemed to have passed since I'd last caressed the head of a knight or a bishop's miter, but in fact I'd played with my father only a few months before, in the house that was our last refuge. I remembered that suburb of Linz where, under false names, we'd led an equally false life of apparent tranquillity, an ordinary existence of commonplace, everyday habits so relentlessly uneventful that at times, albeit only moments long, we had the illusion of safety. But I wondered how long the fiction could last, for the charges against us seemed lodged in every passerby's glance and every shopkeeper's smile, and even in acts of genuine courtesy. With every ring of the doorbell and every tread of footsteps on the stairs, we were convinced our time had come.

For an enormous sum my father had hired a man named Bauer, a gamekeeper, to arrange for an escape on a scow along the Danube. We were to leave the country in just a few days. My father gave us the news at dinner. He was radiant. He opened an old bottle of Rhine wine. The wine had spoiled, but no one complained. The day passed in apparent serenity. My mother played some pieces from the *Anna Magdalena Notebook* on the piano, and it seemed as though we were out of danger. A warm May evening fell. It was then that my father got the chessboard and suggested we play a game. It had been years. We'd agreed not to play since the day he ceased to be my master, but that night he insisted on challenging me, and we began to play under the faint light of a lamp with a bluish paper shade. We spent hours riveted to that board. My father was losing, and I wasn't sure whether to pretend to fall into his final, desperate trap, when the bell rang, and Bauer came up. He was very pale. Something had gone wrong. He was afraid someone had talked. He never had time to finish. Men from the Gestapo were right behind him.

"Your move."

The words jolted me out of my waking dream. The position on the board came into focus. Once again I wondered what to do: pretend to fall into his feeble, puerile snare or elude it with the move that would bring victory? I hesitated for a moment, but then decided to lose—purely, I admit, out of fear. True, I let myself be defeated elegantly, the game continuing for quite a while, my opponent forced to defend himself vigorously against my rearguard attacks. But I lost the game.

I was sent back to the infirmary, and at nine I fell asleep, but in the middle of the night a kapo woke me and ordered me to follow him. I obeyed in silence. Asking questions would only have annoyed him. We went outside the camp. The heath was lit by a crescent moon. We came upon a small group of men: two SS officers with flashlights and an inmate doubled over in pain. The five of us walked to a thicket of larch trees atop a tiny hill not far from the camp. The inmate was ordered to undress and was summarily tied to a tree trunk. Two flashlights were pointed at him, and for the first time I saw his face and the bruises on his stomach and lower abdomen. Horrified, I tried to avert my eyes but was forced to watch. When I lowered my head, the kapo raised it with a stroke of his rubber club. The prisoner was young, no more than twenty, though so emaciated, so completely reduced to the status of "Mussulman"—a walking skeleton—that ascribing a chronological age to him was a matter of pure convention. You could guess it only from his dark and darting eyes, a boy's eyes in an old man's face. He stood before his torturers and wept, imploring them not to kill him, insisting he'd done nothing. I gathered from the reply of one of the SS men that he'd been accused of stealing an article of clothing. The man who'd just spoken to him now approached him, drew a pistol from its holster, and shot him in the face. The young man's body slumped against the tree trunk and hung there, a wretched bundle of bones suspended from the cords. Little enough was left of him while he lived; in death his body seemed empty, like the carcass of a bird entangled in a net. His task complete, the executioner glanced with distaste at his own boot, on which something had splattered. Cursing, he rubbed it on the prisoner's uniform, which lay in a crumpled heap. When he turned to me, I was afraid I was next, and I must have had a strange expression, because all three of them began to chuckle. They laughed and joked all the way back. We reentered the camp like a merry company of nighttime revelers carrying the drunkest of their number home.

This episode of insensate brutality haunted me for days, unfolding again and again before my eyes. Everywhere I looked I saw his face, for merciless emaciation made us all alike, giving us all the same expression, the same dazed look, the same teeth I'd seen clenched against the shot that was to kill him.

But I couldn't stop wondering why I'd been forced to witness his death. Was it the price they'd decided to make me pay? Another life in exchange for mine, provided I was present and fully aware of the bargain? Of course, it wasn't the first execution I'd seen, but it seemed to have been scripted, so to speak, in my honor. Days passed before I could forget it, for the horror was soon supplanted by horror itself.

I was summoned for a second game, and once again I faced

a difficult choice. My opponent had a winning position, this time deserved, when all at once he made an enormous blunder. Till then he'd played with incontestable mastery, but now he found himself mired in difficulty. My position was dangerous as well, but for other reasons. I stood at a fork: one path led to a winning sequence, the other to a continuation that would end in a draw. I was racked by doubt. Winning would be easy, but could I maintain a submissive attitude in victory? I was afraid to find out, and therefore chose to draw. To my surprise, my opponent betrayed no sign of satisfaction. He hadn't in the first game either. Indeed, he even grimaced in disappointment.

My leg had healed, but I had not been returned to the labor camp. It was now clear I'd been granted special privileges by the high command. I feared I would pay dearly for them.

Perhaps they thought I ought to be given something to do, or maybe they simply wished to remind me I was still in a place of death, but for whatever reason, on the evening of that second game I was once again summoned to witness an execution: the hanging of two inmates on the Appellplatz. The camp orchestra accompanied their final dance. Was I meant to consider that a privilege, too?

The schedule seemed to call for two games a week. Three days passed, and we faced each other in a third game. For me the squares of the board were the last place in the world where I could still feel free, a tiny patch that soon swelled to become a boundless universe. Yet I was forced to do violence to myself, filling my shoes, so to speak, with ballast. My life depended on not letting myself humiliate him. I was careful not to strike too hard and to let myself be struck even knowing I could have parried the blows. But I also had to be careful to make it all seem natural and uncalculated. He was, after all, a master capable of detecting fraud.

I was ashamed of my own play but did what I could to ensure he was satisfied with his. I fell into traps deliberately, accepted what I knew were disadvantageous sacrifices. It was like walking a tightrope. The more beautiful the opportunities I was forced to waste, the harder it was to lose. A self-respecting player seeks to win with white and not to lose with black; I sought to draw with white and let myself be beaten with black. I felt queasy every time I chose a losing sequence. I had to violate my nature, as though forced to renounce my God.

So it was that I allowed myself to be overcome in that third game also. But when I was returned to my block and the prison door swung shut behind me, I was struck by an anxious foreboding that something terrible was about to happen.

As I feared, I was again awakened in the middle of the night. For a moment I thought I saw my father's face, as though he'd come to shake me out of sleep to administer the punishment I deserved for my misdeeds. The impression lasted but an instant. A flashlight held a foot or so from my face cast a blinding glare. Someone shouted that I should rise immediately. I didn't ask where I was being taken. I knew I would find out only too soon.

It was a moonless night, the glimmer of a flashlight providing the only light. The squad escorting me must have included half a dozen men or more, but I could distinguish only shadows in the almost complete darkness. Two of them were joking, presumably at my expense. One of them wondered aloud whether I had ever been to a quail hunt. We stopped in a clearing, where two more SS men were waiting for us. Flashlights had been placed on the ground. All around us was thick darkness, yet I seemed to sense movement, a kind of rustling. There was a whisper like a stifled prayer, though when I looked in the direction from which the noise had come I saw nothing. I thought, perhaps hoped, that it was a figment of my imagination. The night now seemed diaphanous. One patch of ineradicable darkness stood out on the ground, otherwise brushed by a dewy glow. Then and only than did I discern the pit. It was a little more than six feet by nine and not very deep, almost like a natural depression in the earth. In the bottom of the pit were human faces.

Someone turned out the flashlights. It was getting lighter, and with the light came the ever louder call of birds. For a while no one moved, but then an order was given. One of the SS men approached the pit, walked around it, removed the bayonet from his rifle, knelt, and reached into the pit as though using a ladle to stir an enormous cauldron. He was cutting the ropes that bound the prisoners. When he stood and replaced his bayonet, the others came near, pushing me before them. Wailing from the pit was drowned out by the curses of the squad leader, who shouted as loudly as he could that they were all to stand up. Shapes began to disentangle themselves, limbs seeming to re-form into forgotten patterns, bodies rising one by one as though answering the trumpet's blare on the day the Messiah comes. They were ordered to take off what they were wearing. They were—or had once been—women. Four women of indeterminate ages. The man who had released them from their bonds told them they were free to go, urging them to leave as quickly as possible, before he changed his mind. Dumb stupor flickered across the four faces. The order to run as fast as they could was now repeated more menacingly.

Four pale and gesticulating figures emerged from the pit and began to walk, stumbling, falling, picking themselves up, and finally breaking into a nightmare run toward the heath, veiled in dawn's first mist. Safety catches clicked and bullets were chambered. The squad unhurriedly assumed the firing position, waiting just long enough to make the competition sporting. Then the "quail hunt" began.

There was no longer any doubt that the price of my privileged status was too high. Forcing me to witness their methods of extermination was tantamount to involving me. It was a heavy burden on my conscience. But I wondered what the point was. They would not leave an eyewitness alive for long. Did they want to strip me of any possible illusion right from the start? Or was it somehow linked to the chess games? This latter hypothesis seemed increasingly plausible. I imagined it as an attempt to wear me down, to sap my lucidity and deprive me of any capacity for concentration. I was dealing with a player who would stop at nothing to win. I certainly hadn't forgotten what happened in Vienna on the eve of our last encounter before the war. But if this form of torture was meant to destroy my concentration, why was it inflicted after each game, allowing me time to recover before the next, instead of immediately before a contest? If it was in fact connected to our games, it seemed more like a direct consequence than a precautionary measure.

An entire week passed before I was summoned again. The

mere thought of what might happen afterward made the idea of playing chess terrifying to me. It was as though I'd forgotten even the most basic rules of the game. I was brought to the same place. The board was ready, and my opponent seemed veiled in a halo of invincibility. He was unusually polite, even offering me a cigarette.

"How are you today, my dear sir?"

"Not well."

His astonishment was patently excessive. "Really? Why is that? Haven't my orders to treat you with all due respect been obeyed? The food, perhaps? Aren't they giving you enough to eat?"

"I can't complain about the food."

"Perhaps your lodgings aren't conducive to concentration?"

"I couldn't ask for better."

"Well, then!" His voice betrayed a hint of irritation. Clearly he was not about to tolerate sarcasm from a Jew, especially a Jew in my position. Yet I hadn't spoken sarcastically. It wasn't that I could imagine nothing better; I couldn't imagine anything at all.

I therefore came right to the point. "They've been waking me up at night," I said.

"Who's been waking you up at night, my dear sir? Your own evil thoughts, perhaps?"

"I don't know. Maybe the men of the Kommando."

"And why are they doing that?"

"They order me to go with them to witness murders."

He was silent for a moment, as though seeking the right words to share a deep secret with me. "I don't think your game is what it used to be," he finally said. "It has somehow declined."

"I don't understand."

"You will, my dear sir, you will," he suddenly blurted, revealing an animosity he'd so far managed to control. "You see, it was I who sent those men."

I still didn't understand.

"My dear sir, if anyone could ever boast of having deceived me, I can assure you it would not be a Jew. Ah, your race! Incredibly sly, aren't you? You pretend not to understand, but I simply cannot believe that a few short months of the harsh discipline of this camp has turned you into the worst sort of dilettante. Be advised, my dear sir, that if I spared your life, it was only because I expected to face an opponent worthy of his reputation. You cannot toy with me. I won't stand for it. You could have won the first game. You deliberately drew the second. Of the third I will not even speak."

I objected with all the strength I had left. "It's not true," I shouted. "I'm not myself in this place. I have no strength or concentration or dignity. I can't play as I used to with all this going on."

For a moment he seemed to take my protest seriously. He came closer and walked around me, staring at my head like a barber examining the results of his labor. He seemed curious about something in the shape of my skull.

"You see, my dear sir, ever since we met, I have wondered which of us is the better player. Back then, if memory serves, we were both considered probable challengers for the world title. Granted, we had a long way to go, but the possibilities were good. Unfortunately, historic events deprived us of our common passion. Your career was ruined—and so was mine. When I discovered that you were here in this camp, I took it as a sign of fate. Finally, I told myself, we will have a chance to test our strength. But I knew the disparity of circumstances would invalidate the contest. That's why I issued orders that you be given the necessary nourishment. As you will have no doubt noticed, I even exempted you from physical labor. Yet one doubt remained: could I count on your complete desire to win, or would you yield to the temptation to flatter me by playing beneath your level, simply to guarantee yourself a life of comfort? I therefore decided that we required a stake. Whoever puts up a stake, no matter how small, cannot permit himself the luxury of sloppy play."

"I don't see what stake I could possibly put up."

"And that's where you're wrong, my dear sir. You've been putting up a stake all along." He seemed amused by my astonishment and struck an arrogant air, as though compelled to resort to a parable to explain a philosophical principle to a half-wit. "Let me tell you a story about the game." He sat down in his armchair and crossed his legs, anticipating the pleasure he would draw from his tale.

"One day a country squire visiting his holdings came upon two louts playing cards, betting with dried beans instead of money. He asked whether the beans were being used as chips, in other words, whether they stood for money. The louts replied that no, they were ordinary beans. 'But what's the point of playing for dried beans?' the squire exclaimed. 'These beans are all we have,' the louts replied."

He paused to give me time to think.

"Now, you know very well that I never play without a stake.

Even if it's only symbolic, it must somehow represent a loss for the loser. I wondered what stakes to propose here, inasmuch as you possess nothing but the coin I gave back to you. Once you lost that, you'd be wiped out. Or do you think you possess something other than that pfennig?"

"No," I replied.

"Are you sure?"

"I still have my life."

"Correct: your life. Don't think that didn't occur to me. Life, too, is an excellent stake. Very romantic, to play for your life. But I would lose my opponent with his first defeat. Unless you have nine lives, like a cat." He chuckled, waiting a futile moment to see if I'd appreciate the joke. "I confess, my dear sir, that at one point I felt I was near a solution. Apart from your life, I said to myself, you also possess a body, with ten fingers, ten toes, two ears, two eyes, a nose, and several other appendages. Why not? It was tempting. I got the idea from *The Merchant of Venice*. The pound of flesh? I even discussed it with the camp doctor, who was enthusiastic. Given proper medical attention, there'd be no risk of infection, and the healing, in strictly clinical terms, would be fairly rapid. I rejected the idea only because it would have forced me to forgo your presence during the periods of, shall we say, convalescence, subsequent to your 'losses.' And of course I would not be able to boast of having played against a . . . whole opponent." He laughed again. "But most of all it would not have been fair, since we wouldn't be putting up stakes of equal value. However much I might have offered, even coins of the purest gold would have had less value for you then those dried beans. But then at last I had a flash of enlightenment. What a fool I'd been not to think of it earlier. There *was* something we both possessed in great abundance and could both place on the table, though admittedly each of us would ascribe a different value to the stakes."

At that point he opened a drawer of his desk and handed me an envelope, which I took and turned over in my hands. On the outside he'd written: "That you might think better."

"You may go now," he said. An SS man came in to escort me. I opened the envelope as we walked along the no-man's-land near the barbed wire. It contained photographs, faces of people I was sure I didn't know. On the back of each picture was the first and last name, place and date of birth, and date of death. The latter dates were recent, coinciding with our games. Suddenly I recognized the eyes of the man I'd seen tied to a tree and murdered with a pistol shot in the face, the first execution they'd made me witness.

Only then did I understand what he meant when he said there was a stake we both could wager; only then did I understand that we'd been playing for human lives, lives that in Bergen-Belsen were worth less than a pfennig, less than a handful of dried beans.

That was when our match began. It was played under the London rules of 1927, like the Alekhine-Capablanca championship: the first to score six victories would be the winner. Draws would not count.

The choice of condemned prisoners (the stakes) would be made from a list of inmates in good enough health that their death would not be a boon to them. For games ending in a draw the list would be ignored; each victory of his would be followed by the death of a number of prisoners that would rise geometrically at each step, as it already had for the first three games. With each of his defeats I would be permitted to erase equal numbers of names from the list. These would be excluded from the game, their lives thereby spared (at least for the moment).

It was a merciless struggle that lasted all winter. Though played on another planet, it had all the features of a match for the world title, the goal each of us had set for himself in bygone times.

It was during this match that I developed my variation. Between games my opponent had ample time to study strategies to stem my counterattack, but its potential remained boundless. The ultimate end of the chain that began centuries ago and stretched to this crucial moment of our story was now clear to me, and it was exactly this *responsibility* that enabled me to recover all my strength in that crisis. If ever I played with every cell of my body, with my soul and my heart, with the weight of the memory of all past generations bearing down on me, it was during that endless match in the winter of 1944. But one thing is certain: it consumed the full power of my imagination. If ever my mind was capable of creating anything original, it was then. But if that challenge no doubt deserves a place in the catalogue of human aberrations, it will not hold such a place in the history of chess. No enthusiast who ran through the same moves today would ever suspect that with these moves men contended, not for fame or fortune, but for the lives of other men.

The challenge produced many draws and ended in my victory. But I suffered two defeats, and for that I was forced to witness the death of twenty-four prisoners, who surely never suspected that their fate was sealed on a chessboard. I still have photographs of all of them, as Hans saw, for those men and women, utterly unknown to me at the time of their death, are bound to me more closely than by any tie of blood. They will dwell in my memory and my consciousness for as long as I live. When I returned to life, I did my best to find the neighborhoods, streets, and houses in which they'd lived, and once each year I tried to make a pilgrimage to all these places.

Liuba Leibowitz, as a child, would sit on the steps of that tailor's shop in Vienna, while Peter Lewitzky stared absently at the sunny square of his Warsaw suburb as he helped his father behind the counter of his drugstore. A tombstone was erected to the presumed remains of Fiona Löwenthal at Beth-Hachajim in Prague . . .

The question I often ask myself is whether I also saved lives. But perhaps it is futile to try to draw such a balance sheet for a place where the living seemed like ghosts of the dead.

I know of only two inmates on the list who definitely escaped death, since I encountered them in Vienna many years after liberation. One was Boris: Boris Snabl, Czechoslovakian, hard of hearing even then, who struck a fearful aspect as a kapo for a time but was relieved of the post when found to be incapable of doing evil. The other, Viennese by birth, worked in the camp tailor shop, where he did well, having been a rag-picker before being interned in Bergen-Belsen. His nickname, Strumpfel Lump, which haunted him for life, was coined by the SS itself. It was he who got us the uniforms for our escape, at the risk of his own life. He knew how to play chess, and one day, having somehow recognized me, he handed me a sack containing a handkerchief-sized chessboard of light and dark patches of coarse cloth sewn together, along with thirty-two buttons of varying sizes, chosen with great care, markings for the pieces crudely scratched into the faces, apparently with a nail.

I learned two things from that conflict. First, that within our minds is a kind of limit beyond which anything is possible, though we always lack the stimulus required to reach it in everyday life. Once I crossed that threshold I became invincible. Nothing could have happened to me. My mind was in the embrace of the Great Adviser, and I ranged over the board as a hawk soars above a field, not the slightest trembling of the smallest leaf escaping his gaze. My opponent was repeatedly subjected to combinations more intricate than any he'd ever seen. However good a player he was, however cold and clever, he groped like a blind man in a bog when faced with my resolve, for he was moving inanimate pieces of wood, while I commanded an array of fearsome golems. I felt as omnipotent as Steinitz when he claimed he could play against God Himself, conceding his opponent a pawn.

The other thing (which I came to understand fully only with the passing years) was that although I won on the chessboard, I was defeated in reality, because from the outset I was an accomplice in a sickening design. The mere fact of remaining alive, an unpunished witness to their murders, coupled me to them, and however much I deluded myself that I'd risen with all my might in defense of my companions, there could be no justification, in the eyes of God or in my own conscience, for the fact that I'd nevertheless played chess for their lives.

■   ■   ■

The slaughter in the Bergen-Belsen camp reached unprecedented proportions that spring. The Allies were just miles away, but the work of extermination showed no sign of halting. The initial order not to leave a single prisoner alive was never rescinded. It was to be carried out as quickly as possible, erasing all evidence before the enemy broke through. Chaos reigned in the camp. Orders were annulled by counterorders in turn annulled by further counterorders. Our persecutors were swept by panic, and desertion was rife. Columns of deportees left the camp for destinations unknown, while ever greater numbers flooded in. The already inadequate food disappeared completely. So many died of starvation that the ovens were overwhelmed. Long ditches were dug, but even these were not enough. Corpses were scattered everywhere, stacked wherever they would fit. When the Allies entered the camp, they found thousands of unburied bodies. But the true dimensions of the slaughter could be guessed only when they found the personal effects confiscated from prisoners on their arrival and preserved with meticulous care: mountains of eyeglasses and caps, hair clips, bracelets, and buttons—things that remained only because they had no value. To this day I sometimes wonder if rich society ladies suspect that hair from murdered women is woven into their fashion wigs, and that their precious necklaces contain melted-down gold taken from teeth ripped from corpses.

As I sat in the Red Cross truck that carried me away from Bergen-Belsen, finally free of my filthy uniform and dressed in clean civilian clothing bearing no insignia of disgrace, I realized that somewhere, in a dimension beyond my ken, a chess game had been played whose stakes and losses were incalculable. I was stupefied that the natural world had emerged indifferent and unscathed, that there was still a month of May like those of my childhood. The sun was no longer darkened by smoke from the ovens of the crematoria, and a breeze swept the sparse shrubs of heather among the low-lying dunes of the Lüneburg heath.